DEATH OF AN OLD GIT

In the village of Castle Farthing a mean-spirited, spiteful, curmudgeonly old man is found drugged and strangled in his cottage, with no obvious clues to the perpetrator of the crime. DI Falconer and Acting DS Carmichael are summoned from the police headquarters in the nearby town of Market Darley and begin to uncover a web of grudges against the old man. As the heat of July continues relentlessly, tempers flare, disturbing the usual rural calm of the village, and the normally imperturbable Harry Falconer. Faced with a crime with no obvious prime suspect, he feels that he is gradually losing his grip on the case as the body count rises...

DEATH OF AN OLD GIT

by

Andrea Frazer

Magna Large Print Books
Long Preston, North Yorkshire,
BD23 4ND, England.

British Library Cataloguing in Publication Data.

A catalogue record of this book is
available from the British Library

ISBN   978-0-7505-4484-9

First published in Great Britain by Accent Press 2013

Published in Large Print 2017 by arrangement with
Accent Press Ltd.

Magna Large Print is an imprint of Library Magna Books Ltd.

Printed and bound in Great Britain by
T.J. (International) Ltd., Cornwall, PL28 8RW

DRAMATIS PERSONAE

<u>The Residents of Castle Farthing</u>

Cadogan, Martha – retired schoolmistress
Covington, George and Paula – licensees of
    The Fisherman's Flies
Lowry, Kerry (née Long) –
    ex-wife of Mike Lowry
Lowry, Michael – owner of the village garage
Malpas-Graves, Brigadier Godfrey, and Joyce –
    of The Old Manor House
Manningford, Piers – IT consultant, married to:
Manningford, Dorothy – interior designer
Morley, Reginald – an unpleasant old man
Rollason, Rebecca, and Nicholas, son Tristram –
    run the village tea-shop
Romaine, Cassandra – artist, married to Clive
Swainton-Smythe, Rev Bertram – vicar,
    married to Lillian
Warren-Browne, Alan and Marian –
    run the village post office
Wilson, Rosemary – runs the village shop,
    Allsorts

<u>The Officials</u>

Detective Inspector Harry Falconer

Acting Detective Constable 'Davey' Carmichael
PC John Proudfoot
Sergeant Bob Bryant
Dr Philip Christmas

Prologue

I

The village of Castle Farthing drowsed in the heat of the July sunshine, postcard-pretty with its diamond-shaped green duck pond and Saxon church.

At the top of the High Street, at the Old Manor House, Brigadier Malpas-Graves scratched his head and frowned as he surveyed the empty patches in his asparagus beds. He was sure and certain that they had not cut that much over the last few days. From the soft fruit beds his wife's voice called, 'There's hardly a strawberry here, and I know there were more raspberries on these canes yesterday. Have you checked the hens?'

'I have indeed,' replied her husband. 'Only the two eggs, and I'm sure it wasn't a fox made off with that bantam the other week. If it was, there would've been feathers and injured birds. I'm going to have to put a stop to this before it gets out of hand.'

'Oh, Godfrey, must you? You know how I hate bad feeling between neighbours.'

'I'm sorry, Joyce, but I must. We're not a charity and I won't be taken for a fool. It has to stop now.' So saying, the Brigadier smoothed down the ends of his white moustache, hitched his belt over his prominent frontage and marched off to check his salad beds.

II

To the west, at The Old School House in Sheep-wash Lane, the white-haired figure of Martha Cadogan could be seen bobbing about in the garden as she twitched out chickweed and other invading greenery from amongst her beloved blooms. Really, she thought as she weeded, these raised beds that Bertie built for me are a real God-send. Nowhere nearly so much bending, and the stonework is really very attractive. She stopped for a minute and smiled as she thought of all the hard work put in by her beloved nephew-in-law, then, spotting greenfly on her rose bushes, resolved to give them a good spray before she set off for her Sunday afternoon stroll, a habit that eased the ache of her arthritis and gave her much-needed contact with the other folk of the village. Since her retirement from teaching she missed the daily hustle and bustle of social intercourse, and did what she could to get out and about and keep up with what was going on in what she considered to be 'her patch'.

III

Next door to her property was an unusual oval-shaped thatched property, appropriately named 'The Beehive' as it boasted several of these in its rear garden. With its whitewashed walls and

10

black-painted window frames and door it had a very attractive appearance which would not have looked out of place on the top of a jigsaw-puzzle box. To the rear of the property, beyond the hives and abutting the orchard wall of 'The Rookery', stood an outbuilding that served as a studio. Inside, Cassandra Romaine was just laying down her paintbrush as her husband Clive appeared in the doorway.

'I've got to nip into the office to get some paperwork for tomorrow. Do you want to come with me for the ride?'

'No thanks. I've got a bit more to do here, then I thought I'd go for a walk to clear my head. You go on. I'll see you at teatime.' As the door closed she picked up her brush again and frowned at the canvas on the easel. It was always so difficult to know just when something was finished.

IV

On the corner of Sheepwash Lane and the High Street, in the substantial residence known as Pilgrims' Rest, Piers Manningford was pacing impatiently round the drawing room, occasionally glancing at his watch and sighing. His wife, Dorothy, at forty-nine eight years his senior, looked up from her laptop and tutted. 'Oh for heaven's sake, Piers, isn't there something you could be doing? I've got to get the design for this warehouse conversion finished today and you're driving me to distraction.'

'Sorry, dear. I wasn't thinking.' He glanced at

his watch again. 'I think I'll just go for a stroll down the Carsfold Road and see if the hang gliders are up, if that's all right with you.'

'Go, go, and give me a bit of peace and quiet. And don't hurry back. I'll be glad to see the back of you for a couple of hours.'

Piers's bored expression dissolved as he headed for the hall to collect his binoculars, stopping at the hallstand to check his already immaculate appearance.

V

In Jasmine Cottage, in the High Street opposite the village green, Kerry Long was on her way out into the back garden to bring in her washing. Sunday was the one day of the week when she did not work, and she liked to keep up to date with her household chores. The cottage was one of a thatched terrace of six, in the past home to the workers on the land that used to be Manor Farm. The land had been sold off in parcels since the last war, first by the Brigadier's father, then by the Brigadier himself, in an effort to afford the upkeep and maintenance of The Old Manor House. Where once there had been cows and crops, now there was a trout farm and fishery, a caravan park and a small development of modern houses. The terrace housing Jasmine Cottage and a similar terrace of six in Drovers Lane had since ceased to be tied cottages and had, likewise, been sold off to bolster the coffers of 'the big house'.

Kerry's smile of approval at her brilliant white

sheets moving in the slight breeze turned to a grimace of disgust as she noticed a brown stain in the centre of the folded double sheet. Her gaze moved down to the ground, to the path below the washing line, where lay the culprit, a misshapen but nevertheless recognisable lump of dog dirt. Her temper began to rise. Many a time she had suspected that her next door neighbour had encouraged his Jack Russell to push its way through the hedge to do his business in her garden, and scratches in the herbaceous borders had argued the accuracy of her suspicions. This, however, was entirely different. Buster could not have made that mark: it was a good three feet from ground level. The 'missile' had been aimed and thrown, calculated to smear the largest item on the clothesline, the most awkward to rewash, for she boasted no washing machine.

Turning to shoo her two children back indoors so that she could safely dispose of the health hazard, she leaned over the fence, her anger getting the better of her. 'Are you in there you malicious old sod? Don't think I don't know what you've done. Well, you're not getting away with it any more. I've had you and your twisted mind up to here. It's about time something was done about you, so take fair warning that I'm the one who's going to do it.'

VI

That 'old sod', aka Reginald Morley, sat in a battered old Windsor chair in the kitchen next door in Crabapple Cottage, and wheezed the asthmatic laugh of an elderly smoker. At his feet Buster twitched in his sleep, as the shrill voice from next door berated his master. Reg was greatly cheered, not just by the accuracy of his shot, but at the reaction it had produced. A wizened old man, long past his eightieth birthday, he seemed to have shrunk, dried out, and gone bad like an old plum since his wife had died. They had not been able to have children of their own, and his wife's bitterness at this misfortune had turned him against children in general. In his wife's lifetime it had been just a fairly mild aversion, but since her death it had turned to open hostility. Since Kerry Lowry and what he mentally referred to as 'those two mewling, snotty-nosed brats' had moved next door he had made it his life's mission to make all their lives a misery. Every little victory, every point scored, he hugged to himself in silent glee and added to his twisted treasury of sour memories.

VII

In St Cuthbert's parish church, opposite the village green on the eastern fork of the Carsfold Road, the Reverend Bertie Swainton-Smythe was stacking hymn books at the rear of the church. He was a tall man in his early fifties, just beginning to run to fat. Generally good-humoured and easy-going, with a slight twinkle in his hazel eyes, he was considered by the village to be a good man to have around in a crisis.

14

His mop of thick brown hair bobbed back and forth as he bent to his task. Matins and the Eucharist were over and, as it was the third Sunday of the month, there would be no Evensong. Business was over for the day, as it were. The coarseness of the expression made him wince, and a vision of his wife popped involuntarily into his conscious thoughts. Although he loved her dearly, he sometimes wished she could be a little more like her Aunt Martha in her ways: a little more genteel, a little more ladylike. Bertie sighed, recognising a prayer to St Jude when he heard one, and continued with his monotonous task.

At the front of the church Lillian Swainton-Smythe was rearranging the floral displays, removing faded blooms and redistributing greenery to try to get a few more days out of them before they needed to be discarded and replaced with fresh ones. Less than a year younger than her husband, she was the complete antithesis to him in temperament, tending towards the hyperactive, even the manic; she was very outspoken, and gave a good impression of a headless chicken when faced with any sort of crisis. She was short of stature and, like Bertie, becoming slightly tubby. Her eyes were blue; her hair a thick, shoulder-length style, highlighted to disguise the influx of grey that had invaded her tresses over the past few years. She was the perfect foil for her husband: they balanced each other out nicely because of their differences.

'Oh, to hell with these flowers! They'll keep till the morning,' she muttered to herself then, raising her voice, called, 'How about we call it a day, Bertie? Fancy a G and T?'

Slipping the final hymn book back into place, her husband called back, 'Lovely, but just the one. I've got to pop out later.'

VIII

Even though it was high summer, the Castle Farthing Teashop was shut for a few hours, its owners next door in The Rookery enjoying a rare family moment together. As it was such a beautiful day, Tristram Rollason (aged fourteen months) was out and about in the garden, sampling woodlice, daisies and other such outdoor delicacies. He had very magnanimously agreed to his parents joining him on this Sunday treat, and they reclined now in sun loungers sipping iced lemonade, occasionally chatting, but mainly watching the antics of their beloved first-born.

The Rollasons were in their late twenties, both born locally. A tall man with blue eyes and light brown hair, Nicholas could definitely be described as a strong, silent, traditional Englishman. On weekdays he worked for an insurance company in Carsfold. Rebecca was a tall, solid country girl with dark hair, green eyes and a smile of dazzling beauty. Tristram looked the image of his father until he smiled, when he became an angel.

Rebecca had had the (good) luck to be made redundant from her job just before she discovered she was pregnant. This proved a blessing in disguise, as the redundancy money helped them pay for the lease on the teashop, and meant that Rebecca could continue to work after Tristram was born, but had no need to leave her baby with someone else to do so. Life could hardly have been more perfect for the little family. There was only one fly in their ointment and Nicholas had resolved to squash that insect.

'I've been asking around and it's got to be him. You know what a nuisance he was when we were courting. I'm going to face him with it. It has to stop now.'

'I wish you wouldn't, Nick. I should have remembered to draw the curtains. It's not as if we live in the middle of nowhere. I should've thought.'

'Curtains, be blowed. That's our own back garden out there. I'm going to speak to him about this, for if it happens again I'll not be held responsible.'

'Oh, Nick!'

'Well...'

'That's that, then. Good. Oh no, look at the time! I'll have to get my skates on if we're to be open in time for afternoon teas.'

IX

Next door to the teashop the CFFC (Castle Farthing Farmers' Co-operative) was closed for business. Run by a couple, both the offspring of local farmers, they preferred to spend their Sundays catching up with the fascinating developments of family and farming life during the previous week.

Next to this establishment, on the corner of Drovers Lane, the general store, 'Allsorts', stayed open for those dilatory few who ran out of gravy browning, or who had forgotten to buy eggs. Rosemary Wilson, who ran the shop, considered Sunday opening not so much a commercial exercise as an example of social work.

As she served her few customers, the sound of banging and metal-cutting drifted across from the workshop at the rear of Castle Farthing Garage in Drovers Lane. Rosemary sighed. That boy was working on a Sunday again, when he couldn't find five minutes to spend with his own kiddies. If he could not find the time, at least all this extra work ought to make him enough money so that he didn't fall behind with his maintenance payments.

X

The sound of metal on metal also reached the walled garden of the post office, where Alan and Marian Warren-Browne were sitting in the shade of a venerable tree. Alan set down his teacup and frowned.

'I hope that racket doesn't start off that damned dog next door.'

'Oh, I shouldn't think so,' opined his wife, although her expression was an anxious one. 'We heard nothing from him when Kerry was calling for the old man a while ago. Maybe they're having a nap, or even out somewhere.'

The clang-clanging and grinding of metal on metal continued unabated.

XI

At The Fisherman's Flies, Castle Farthing's only hostelry, George and Paula Covington may not have been in the first, or even second, flush of youth, but they could have taught today's young quite a bit about the execution and enjoyment of a little bit (or even a lot) of 'afternoon delight'. They anticipated it eagerly as they finished clearing away the last of the lunchtime debris.

Chapter One

Sunday 12th July – afternoon and evening

I

From where she stood, feeding the ducks on the village green, old Martha Cadogan could see George Covington outside the public house, collecting glasses, as his wife Paula followed behind emptying ashtrays and collecting carelessly discarded crisp packets. Sunlight glinted off the weathervane atop the tower of St Cuthbert's and the vicar, husband of Martha's niece Lillian, greeted her as he cycled past on some unknown errand.

Castle Farthing, with the exception of the surfeit of motorised through-traffic, had changed little since Martha was a girl. Now eighty-five, she reflected on the whole of a lifetime spent in one village, first as a child, then as the schoolmistress, and now, when no doubt she was known as 'that old biddy from Sheepwash Lane'. A dazzle of bright colour lit the periphery of the old lady's vision and she turned slightly to observe the village's artist, Cassandra Romaine, swanning her way down the High Street, her outfit a rainbow of dip-dyed cheesecloth and vivid scarves. With a wave of her hand the younger woman turned left into Church Street, leaving the afternoon somehow cooler and less bright.

Across the green the Covingtons had ceased to dart around the umbrella-shaded tables of The Fisherman's Flies, and were taking a break to chat to a figure that Martha easily identified (for her eyesight was still sharp, despite her years) as Piers Manningford, an incomer who, it seemed, was doing his best to integrate into village life, despite a deeply felt desire to keep himself to himself most of the time. He seemed to be making a real effort. Perhaps he was just shy, she thought.

From a window in the Castle Farthing Teashop a white tea towel appeared and was shaken vigorously. It was soon replaced with a head that yodelled 'toodle-oo' across the green. Martha acknowledged young Rebecca Rollason with a wave, and watched with amusement as young Tristram toddled unsteadily out of the teashop door, only to be scooped up within six steps, and carried, bawling in protest, back into the cool, safe interior.

Hearing the yapping of a dog behind her, she turned to see Reg Morley, nearly as old as her, only a couple of years behind her at school, emerge from the musty interior of Crabapple Cottage with his Jack Russell. As he bent to clip on the little dog's lead, a head emerged from an upstairs window next door in Jasmine Cottage to issue an ultimatum. 'You just make sure that mangy mutt of yours does his business while you're out and doesn't save it up for my back garden later.' Muttering under his breath, old man and dog set off to see what sport the afternoon had to offer, Reg pulling viciously on the lead when the dog veered off in excitement at an interesting scent.

Martha Cadogan, having exhausted her supply of stale bread on the ducks who resided at the village pond, sat down on the bench next to the war memorial to watch the continuation of the Castle Farthing Sunday afternoon perambulations, in the hope of a conversation or two. The fair weather currently prevailing boded well for St Swithin's Day on the fifteenth, and thus the superstitious promise of fair weather to come should prove a good opening gambit.

Shadows were beginning to lengthen when the squeak of the church gate announced that either someone had mistakenly turned up for Evensong, or the shortcut from the woods had been selected in preference to going round the long route on the Carsfold Road.

As the catch caught with a 'snick', a still-energetic Buster bounded round his master's feet, slowing the old man's already arthritic progress to a funereal crawl. Reg Morley did not seem to notice the joyous capering of his pet, as he looked alternately cunning and confused, even stopping at one point, at the corner of Church Street and the High Street, to raise the greasy peak of his ancient flat cap and give a tentative scratch at his head with a grimy, broken-nailed finger, as he stood contemplating something in the middle distance. A perplexed smile creased his forehead as he muttered to himself, 'I knowed that one. I'd've knowed that voice anywhere. That other though – can't place it. But who'd've thought it. Dirty buggers!'

Finally rousing himself from this reverie, he gave a sharp tug on the dog's lead and, getting no response, used his foot to gain attention, before heading the few yards to his own front door, whistling softly to himself, half a twinkle forming in his age-dimmed, rheumy eyes.

Even if the old man had realised that this was to be his last day on this earth, he would still have been surprised at what a busy and informative evening he would pass, before leaving this vale of tears to meet his maker. Oblivious to what was to occur over the next few hours, Reg Morley lit the gas under his old tin kettle, switched on the radio, and opened the back door to let Buster out to run off the last of his energy before bedtime. The action was about to commence as fate marched inexorably towards his shabby abode.

II

Castle Farthing is a smallish village, too far east to be deemed in the 'West Country', and too far west to be considered a part of the south-east. A small-ish village in an area of many such small-ish villages, it occupies an enviable position in a shallow valley bordered, on the north, by a stream and the ruins that gave it its name, and, to the south, by agricultural land and woods. Farms also line the roads leaving Castle Farthing to east and west.

As far as small-ish villages go, it can afford to be slightly smug, as it is on the picturesque side. A diamond-shaped village green at its centre is home to a duck pond, a war memorial, several venerable oak trees, and two benches, where passers-by can sit and enjoy a shady umbrella of leaves in the summer.

The Carsfold Road enters the village from roughly due south, and forks around the lower half of the green's diamond. To the right, an obtuse angle is formed, with Church Street leading to St Cuthbert's parish church (Saxon tower, Norman font, and unusual sarcophagi in the churchyard), the vicarage and the village hall. The left-hand lower section of Castle Farthing houses its only pub, The Fisherman's Flies, a petrol station and an occasional doctors' surgery.

A casual visitor wandering north up the High Street which, a few short steps ago, had been the Carsfold Road, might be momentarily disconcerted by the simultaneous change of road name on both sides of the green. (New postmen were driven to distraction by the proliferation of quaint house names, and the eccentric numbering system that had developed, like a separate life-form, over the years.)

The north-western quarter of the village, now being passed through by our imaginary visitor, possesses Castle Farthing's few shops – a general store, a farmers' cooperative, and a tea shop. At

23

the very top of this corner of the village, where the stream weaves lazy coils through the vale, is a trout farm. The remaining quarter houses a post office, a terrace of ramshackle thatched cottages, picturesque to look at but uncomfortable to live in, and The Old Manor House.

To the rear of the grandly-proportioned Old Manor is the ugly scar of a new housing development, and a caravan park occupying some of the land that used to belong to the big house, since sold off for the upkeep of an elaborate, draughty and inconvenient residence, which also just happens to be the best address in the village.

III

Reg Morley didn't give a fig for picturesque, so long as life was interesting, and today had been extremely interesting. Settling in a grubby armchair, he replayed its highlights in an imaginary video, from the 'interesting' eavesdropping in the woods earlier – interesting and, maybe, profitable, if only he could get it properly figured out in his head – to the three extremely satisfying arguments he had enjoyed since returning home. Buster's whining interrupted these thoughts, and he realised that the dog had some last-minute business to conduct. On a whim, the old man decided to take him out the front, see if he could not get the dog to leave someone a little present for the morning. Then he might shut him out for a bit. The kiddies next door would be asleep by now, and a bit of hearty yapping should give that cheeky mother of theirs the run-around for a while, trying to resettle them.

As he stood outside the post office in the gathering dusk, holding the lead of an obliging Buster, a flash of colour caught his eye. A red or brown would have gone unnoticed in the fading light, but this vivid turquoise was almost arrogant in its brightness. As Buster gave a single yap to indicate the end of his 'business', a penny dropped in old Reg's brain. And as the penny dropped, a devious smile spread across his sour features. And, as he smiled, the figure turned and looked directly at him. Reg raised his free hand and waved lazily. He could afford to be magnanimous because, now he did have everything figured out, he could concentrate on how to extract the maximum profit and the maximum fun from that knowledge. He had them both bang to rights, one by the voice; the other, by the clothing.

Reg Morley had never in his life heard the word *Schadenfreude*, and now he never would, which was a pity since he had revelled in it for all but the first two or three years of his miserable, bitter life. Giving a harsh tug on the lead that set Buster whining, he half-dragged the little dog back through the front door of his cottage. Martha Cadogan, passing on the other side of the green on her way home from supper with her niece and nephew-in-law, averted her gaze at this unnecessarily harsh treatment of a dumb animal.

The last sliver of the setting sun slipped below the skyline, and the serene orb of a full moon glided into prominence to gild the rooftops of this typical, peaceful English village.

25

Chapter Two

Monday 13th July – morning

I

The mist heralding a fine Monday had already dispersed in wraiths and ribbons, and the sun sparked diamond fire from pond and stream. Even at this early hour, when Castle Farthing was just beginning to stir and shrug off the sluggishness of sleep, a haze shimmered from the roads, and the village cats, ever vigilant in the pursuit of their own comfort, sought shade where they could.

Commuters and agricultural workers had long left for their labours as the local children congregated at the war memorial to await the arrival of the school bus, and the commercial section of the High Street drew its bolts and opened its doors for another day's trade. No chimney smoked to cloy the sweet summer air, most houses had their windows flung wide, and doors were propped wide open with an ingenious range of improvised doorstops: here a hefty flint, there an inverted floor mop.

In the small sorting office at the rear of the post office, Alan and Marian Warren-Browne were putting in order the letters and packets for the first delivery of the day. Alan's short frame was hunched over the table, his small hands furiously rifling through and extracting those items for outlying properties that would need delivery by van. His lips moved in a silent litany of addresses and, occasionally, he winced and rubbed at his back when he had bent uncomfortably far to reach an envelope.

Opposite him, his wife's waif-like figure worked more slowly, almost ponderously, as she assembled the on-foot deliveries for the main village. Every couple of minutes she would slow to a halt, raise a birdlike hand to brush her mousy fringe from her eyes, and wipe away the thin film of perspiration that had formed on her forehead.

In the background, constantly, came the yapping that could only be Buster. On and on it went, although slightly muffled, which must mean that Reg could not be bothered to let him out into the garden to be about his morning 'business'. That was a mixed blessing, for the barrier of the back door muted the sound a little and, if let out, the volume of the staccato yelps would increase. Then again, they might just stop completely given the little dog's joy at being abroad in the fresh air.

With a quick glance at the wall clock, Alan snapped an elastic band round the last of his letters, and rose to open the front door to any early customers. As he ducked through the low doorway, Marian ceased her sorting altogether and raised both hands to cradle her head. The dog's frantic entreaties bit into her brain like needles: she could feel the fire in her head about to ignite. A silent tear rolled down her cheek, and she was too sunk in her own misery to hear her husband's sharp cry of disgust and his bustling return, his right shoe in his hand, held at arm's length.

'Just one step outside,' he explained, heading for the minute kitchen area where they made their tea and coffee when on duty. 'Just one step and I was in it. He takes that damned dog through the woods every day and he's got a perfectly good garden of his own, so why does that yappy little tripe-hound of his always do its business by our front door? One of those two is evil, and I doubt it's the dog,' he continued, mopping with kitchen roll and sprinkling disinfectant. 'I wouldn't put it past that old codger to have trained the dog somehow, got it to poo to order, just where he wants it to. He's upset just about everyone in this village and I, for one, have...'

He trailed to a halt as he returned to the sorting area and saw his wife's waxen face beaded with sweat and streaked with tears. 'Have you got another migraine?' Marian nodded carefully and winced. 'Is it that damned dog again?' (Another careful nod.) 'Well, that's the last straw. I'm going round now to give him a piece of my mind, and if he doesn't do something this time about that bloody animal, there just might be a nasty accident in the woods come pheasant shooting season.' Alan fantasised about meting out a swift end to his canine adversary. *Terribly sorry, Your Honour. There was a movement in the grass, he was off the lead and, well he is – was – such a small dog. Easy mistake to make in the heat of the moment.* It'd be worth the day in court just for the peace and quiet.

And with that, the postmaster disappeared. A few seconds later Marian heard a furious, 'Oh, *no!* I can't believe I've trodden in it again. Well, he'll just have to have it on his carpets and serve him right.' The door slammed shut and she was left with just the dog's yaps and her pain for company.

II

From the window of the Castle Farthing Teashop, Rebecca Rollason held up her small son and pointed across the green. 'Look at cross old Mr Warren-Browne banging on nasty Mr Morley's door,' she crooned. 'Doesn't he look funny with his face all red? He looks very, very cross to me.' Tristram gurgled his approval of this impromptu entertainment, and she continued, 'What's he going to do now, then? Naughty Mr Morley must be hiding 'cause he doesn't want to answer the door. Ah, cross old Mr Warren-Browne's going down the side now. He's going to surprise naughty Mr Morley at the back door. I don't think naughty Mr Morley will like that, do you, precious? But we don't care, because naughty Mr Morley is a dirty old man, and Daddy says he's going to punch him on the snoot one of these fine days.'

A muted banging sounded from the rear of Crabapple Cottage. 'Let's go sit outside for a minute, shall we, baby? Then we can hear better if the naughty men are going to shout at each other, and it doesn't matter if they use bad words, because you won't understand them, will you, my little bundle of joy?' She settled her son on her hip and stepped out into the High Street, ears strained for the expected slanging match.

But there came no shouting. Even the dog's

29

yapping ceased, leaving a silence that was almost painful to the ears.

Rebecca's pretty face creased in a frown, then her eyes and mouth became so many Os, as Alan Warren-Browne reappeared, this time through the front door, face now white, hair standing on end where he had raked his fingers through it in disbelief. Catching sight of Rebecca, he lurched towards the green calling hoarsely, 'Police. Call the police. 999. Someone's done for the old bugger. He's as dead as a doornail.'

III

About seven miles to the north of Castle Farthing lies the town of Market Darley. As market towns go, it is quite pretty, with a weathered market cross, a sprinkling of churches, a couple of supermarkets, and a large selection of the small, idiosyncratic shops that seem to congregate in towns of this ilk. It has a town hall, a cottage hospital, a hotel, four public houses and a limited range of the other necessary amenities. As it is the only place in the area that can be dignified with the name 'town', and as it is fairly central to the area's villages, it also has a decent-sized police station which, at this moment, is running at minimum strength, mainly due to the number of officers fighting German tourists for sunbeds round pools in a variety of sunny locations.

In an office, to the rear of the first floor in this police station, sits a man painstakingly re-shaping a ragged fingernail on an otherwise immaculately manicured hand. His hair is dark, short and straight; his eyes are dark and his skin is tanned; he is within six months of his fortieth birthday. Today, he is wearing an exquisitely-cut lightweight beige suit, a cream shirt, and a tie of pale pink silk; his socks are cream and his brogues brown; a hand-kerchief peeps shyly from his breast pocket. The heat of the day has left him unmoved, and he looks as immaculate as when he had dressed at seven that morning.

At a desk opposite sits another man. Not much more than half the older man's age, he is however nearly twice the size. Six feet five and a half inches in his rather large cotton socks, he is built along the lines of a brick outhouse. Everything about him is untidy. His hair sticks up in sweaty tufts, his tie is askew, his collar open. Ink stains his fingers and he breathes adenoidally through his mouth, as what passes for his brain fights the heat in order to deal with the paperwork before him.

The internal telephone on the older man's desk trills self-importantly and he puts down his nail file and lifts the receiver. 'Yes?' (Pause) 'Speaking.' (Pause) 'Oh, not in another godforsaken village?' (Pause) 'If I must. But who will I take with me? My sergeant's on leave for another week.' (Pause) 'You can't mean that.' (Pause) 'You do mean that.' (Pause) 'A plague on your house, Bob Bryant.'

Inspector Harry Falconer replaced the tele-phone handset and looked across the office with an expression of disdain. 'Come along, Constable Carmichael, you've been seconded to plain clothes and temporarily promoted, so now you're an acting detective sergeant. We've got a murder

31

on our hands so, let's be getting you into some of the aforementioned apparel.'

'Beg pardon, sir?'

'Out of uniform, Carmichael. That's what plain clothes means.' Falconer sighed.

Ralph 'Davey' Carmichael put down the statement he had been making such heavy weather of, his features a picture of awe and delight.

'And it's a real live murder, sir?'

'No, a real dead one. Come on, man, look lively. We've got to get changed.'

'Have we got time to bother with what we're wearing, sir?'

Falconer's upper lip lifted almost imperceptibly in the wraith of a sneer. 'If you think I'm going into the country wearing town clothes you must be mad. Anyway, what's half an hour to a corpse? It'll still be just as dead if we don't turn up till tomorrow. By the way, do you have a car?'

'Skoda,' replied the younger man, eyes now agleam with anticipation.

'We'll take mine.' Falconer drove a sporty little two-seater. As they descended the stairs, he eyed Carmichael's bulk dubiously, and idly wondered if he had a shoehorn in the glove compartment.

IV

Harry Falconer tapped the steering wheel impatiently, as he waited outside the dingy terrace where Carmichael lived with his mother, current step-father and an assortment of siblings and half-siblings. Partly-dismantled motorcycles fought for space with lop-sided tricycles and dolls' prams, amidst the forlorn clumps of weeds and mess that passed for a front garden.

The inspector looked down approvingly at his own fresh attire. His trousers were lightweight twill with a hint of lovat, his shirt lemon, his waistcoat in discreet tweed, and his tie and jacket a muted brown. He looked (and felt) every inch the English country gentleman. But nothing lasts for ever...

Carmichael finally emerged through the debris-strewn frontage in what he considered appropriate attire for the occasion, and Falconer stared in disbelief at the vision of sartorial inelegance that was his partner-in-crime. In place of his rumpled (but at least discreet) uniform, he now wore a pink, orange and green Hawaiian shirt, blue and purple Bermuda shorts, sandals (with regulation black socks), the whole ensemble topped off with an Arsenal baseball cap worn the right way round. Carmichael was probably the only twenty-something person in Market Darley, possibly in the world, who always wore his baseball cap the right way round, a fitting testimonial to his conservative attitude to life (if not to colour co-ordination).

'This do, sir?' he ventured almost shyly.

'Get in quickly, man. Quickly!' Falconer thought, but was too stunned to add, 'Before someone sees you.' An awful lot of people were going to see Carmichael today, and each and every one of them was going to remember who was with him.

V

There is nothing faster-growing known to man (or woman) than that which goes by the name of 'the village grapevine'. The airwaves and the Green were thick with news, rumour and conjecture. Alan Warren-Browne had taken the unprecedented step of closing the post office during normal opening hours, and had retired to his bed where he lay, exhausted with shock, next to his wife who snored gently and peacefully, escaping her migraine with the aid of a sleeping tablet.

Rebecca Rollason's 999 call had initially summoned Constable John Proudfoot from Carsfold, a large village five miles south of Castle Farthing, and it was he who, realising that he was out of his depth, had called for assistance from higher up. His solid figure now guarded the closed front door of Crabapple Cottage. He stood there now, immovable and silent, perspiring gently, secure in the knowledge that he would soon be able to wash his hands of the whole messy situation and get back to some proper rural policing, like sheep-worrying, and possession of unlicensed shotguns. It was a rather muddled thought that made him sound quite criminal, but he knew what he meant, and that was all that mattered.

Lack of solid information did not hinder the growth of the grapevine though, it merely meant that it had to rely more heavily on rumour and conjecture to stretch its spreading tendrils.

At the vicarage Rev. Bertie Swainton-Smythe entered his dank, north-facing study to answer the summons of the telephone. Picking up the receiver

34

he trilled, 'Three, five, seven,' thus immediately declaring himself to be what was known colloquially as 'OV' (as opposed to 'NV'). Many village communities have their petty snobberies and, although not exclusive to it, this was one which Castle Farthing had embraced since telephone numbers ceased to have only three digits.

To elucidate briefly, any resident who had been born in the village, or whose family had lived there for at least a hundred years, and who, furthermore, lived in one of the older properties with an old-style telephone number, was deemed to be Old Village. Anyone who did not fulfil these criteria was deemed to be New Village, including those who had always lived there but had moved to modern houses. Old telephone numbers shared the first three digits: new telephone numbers in the village only shared the first two digits, therefore, NV's had to declare four digits when answering the instrument, or passing on their number to a new neighbour.

The Reverend Bertie himself was, technically, NV as he had only been the incumbent at St Cuthbert's for ten years. Married, however, to Lillian who had been born there, and who was niece to Martha who had, likewise, been born there, he had been tacitly accepted as OV in more than just his telephone number. It must be said, though, that his being a man of the cloth was largely responsible for the warm welcome he received in most villagers' homes.

But, to return to Bertie in his gloomy study: his cheery 'Three, five, seven,' was answered by the voice of his aunt-by-marriage.

'Have you heard, Bertie? Has anyone sent for you yet?'

'Heard what, Auntie?' he asked, a knot of apprehension forming in his stomach.

'About old Reg Morley.'

'What about him?'

'Dead. Murdered.'

'Surely he can't have been murdered, Aunt Martha. Not in Castle Farthing. This is a nice village. People don't get murdered here. It must have been his heart. He wasn't a young man and he did smoke.'

'Bertie, stop rambling and listen to me. When I went down to collect my paper the whole village was buzzing with it. They say that Alan Warren-Browne found him about an hour ago, but he's gone to ground.'

'How did he find him? I mean, how did he know he'd been murdered and hadn't just passed away in his sleep?'

The old lady's voice took on an edge of exasperation. 'How should I know, Bertie dear. All sorts of rumours are flying around. Some say he was in a pool of blood with his head bashed in, some are sure there was a knife in the place where his heart would have been if he'd had one, and others say that he was strangled and robbed. I went to find out what had happened to the poor dog, but that John Proudfoot was standing outside the front door doing a pretty good impression of all three wise monkeys. Why, when I remember how backward he was with his reading, and all the extra time I had to give him, I could slap him for trying to ignore me like that.'

Bertie could easily visualise this encounter, and gave a little smirk, before he recalled the seriousness of the conversation. 'Leave it to me, Auntie. I'll go round right away. After all, I would have been his spiritual advisor, should the old gent ever have felt the need for such a thing,' and with this he hung up the receiver and went in search of his old panama hat as protection against the heat of the sun.

Both benches on the village green were occupied, and a suspiciously large number of people had suddenly been moved to feed the ducks on the pond. In fact, so numerous were they that the ducks had taken fright at the rain of stale bread and dry cake, and had fled, en masse, into the safety of the reeds in the centre of the pond to ride out this unwarranted spell of popularity. The village shops were also doing a surprisingly brisk trade for a Monday morning. Rosemary Wilson and Kerry Long were run off their feet in Allsorts, as were the Heaths in the CFFC. Thirsty hordes filled the teashop and spilled out on to the few tables and chairs outside on the pavement. The air was full of anticipation and the hum of conversation, and all eyes were fixed, some blatantly, some warily, on that lone figure of authority guarding the door of number four High Street, aka Crabapple Cottage.

Chapter Three

Monday 13th July – midday

I

The solemn tolling of a lone bell echoed sonorously across village and fields. Those out and about on the green bowed their heads, some crossing themselves self-consciously. The bell tolled on for Reg Morley. Farmers and labourers in the fields stopped what they were doing, removed their caps and counted to see if the departed was young or old. As the tolls continued they relaxed a little. At least it had not been a child.

It was into this sombre atmosphere that Falconer and Carmichael drove, pulling up just past Crabapple Cottage into a space, coned off by Constable Proudfoot, by the walled garden of the post office. Falconer locked his car and approached the uniformed officer, surprised to find his initial greeting ignored, as the perspiring constable's lips moved silently, counting. 'Seventy-nine, eighty, eighty-one, eighty-two, eighty-three... Sorry, sir. What was that you said?'

'What on earth were you counting for, Constable...?'

'Proudfoot, sir. Constable Proudfoot. Passing bell. I were counting.'

'What in the name of goodness is a passing bell?'

38

'Tells folk that one of their own's passed on. The number of tolls gives their age.'

'Fascinating,' glowered Falconer, who always felt out of his depth when people went all 'harvest home' on him. 'Where's the body?'

'Kitchen, sir.'

'Nothing's been touched, I hope.'

'Well...' Proudfoot looked a mite uncomfortable.

'What do you mean?'

'There's sort of someone with him.'

'Sort of? There can't be "sort of" someone with him. Either there is or there isn't!'

'There is.' Proudfoot's colour was rising with his discomfiture.

'Who? When? Why?' Falconer's high horse had just stepped forward to be mounted.

''Tis only the vicar, sir. Couldn't see no harm in that.'

'Couldn't you, Constable Proudfoot? And what if the vicar is the one who did for this old gentleman, or it was someone he knows and wants to protect. He could be in there now destroying vital evidence, while you stand out here turning a blind eye and aiding and abetting him.'

'But 'tis only the vicar, sir. He wouldn't do nothing like that. He's a man of God.'

'With feet of clay, no doubt. Get out of my way, you bumbling fool, before there's any more harm done.' And, pushing the bulky man to one side, he beckoned to Carmichael (glinting like a jewel in his rainbow attire) to follow him, and bustled through the front door of the cottage, bristling with indignation.

39

'What the hell do you think you're doing, sir?' roared Falconer. The earthly remains of Reg Morley were slumped in a Windsor chair by the range, a man in black kneeling before him, apparently examining his knees.

'Praying for his immortal soul. And who might you be?' asked the vicar, rising from his knees and extending a hand in greeting.

'Inspector Falconer, and this,' (he winced at the shambolic figure ducking under the low ceiling), 'is Acting Detective Sergeant Carmichael. And you are?'

'Vicar of this parish, for my sins. Bertie Swainton-Smythe. D.D.' Their hands met briefly, more of a squaring-up than a tactile social ritual.

'Indeedy?' Falconer already felt wrong-footed.

'No, no. D.D. – Doctor of Divinity. Sorry. Didn't mean to catch you out.'

Oh yeah, sure you didn't, but Falconer kept this thought to himself.

'That bell that was ringing when we got here. Do you always do that?' Carmichael was always eager to learn where he could.

'Oh, yes.' Bertie felt inclined to conversation, now that introductions, however shaky, had been effected. 'Got to keep up all the old customs. The village expects it. We're high church here, you know. Oodles of incense and enough genuflexions to create a surplus – bit of a pun there, I'm afraid: surplus and surplice. We have early communion

40

and sung Eucharist every Sunday, Matins first and third Sundays of the month, Evensong, second and fourth.'

'What about the fifth Sundays?' Falconer cut in, with a sarcastic edge to his voice.

'Practically a day off, old chap, what? Ha ha! Get the old Eucharist out of the way early, and feet up for the rest of the day.' Bertie was oblivious to sarcasm.

'Right, that's enough of this tomfoolery. Let's get on with the job at hand, and stop clucking like a gaggle of old ladies. Vicar, turn out your pockets, and then I want you out of here. This is a crime scene, not a parish knitting circle.'

Left to their own devices, the two policemen had their first opportunity to examine the body, although they could not yet move it, as first the police surgeon had to pronounce the life officially over, and photographs and fingerprints would have to be taken.

Even at first glance, it was fairly obvious that the old man had been garrotted. His empurpled, swollen features supported this, and the fold in his scrawny neck, where whatever had been used to choke the life out of him, was just visible. He was slumped backwards in the wooden chair, his hands hanging over the sides, where they must have fallen when his struggles ceased, and he had lost his fight for life. A dark stain before the range and some shards of china showed where his drumming feet must have kicked a cup over.

'Cocoa,' decided Carmichael, who had dropped to his knees on the grubby floor to sniff the area.

'Well done, lad,' Falconer thanked him grate-

41

fully, eyeing the state of the brick-tiled floor and his own immaculate trousering. 'Let's see if there's anything here for us, any signs of a forced entry, then we'll get started on the neighbours, see if anyone heard or saw anything yesterday evening. We'll assume evening because of the cocoa.'

Even in the heat of summer, a musty, dank smell hung in the air and mingled with the aromas of dog and seldom-washed owner. A fly buzzed lazily at the closed window, no doubt drowsy from the stale air. 'Come on, Carmichael.' Falconer indicated with his head towards the front of the property. 'Let's go and play "Grass Thy Neighbour".'

III

As a young man, Falconer had served ten years in the army, and those years had left their mark. He owed his immaculate appearance and painstaking attention to detail to this era of his life. He had also learnt, during this decade, to 'learn' his enemy before engaging him (or her) in combat. To this end, he would take initial statements from a great number of people at the start of an investigation and, without pressing them on any involvement on their part, would, with gentle encouragement, get them to 'squeal' on anyone they wished. After a little judicious cross-referencing and collation, he would end up with a useful list of accusations with which to begin his second round of statements. It was devious, but it got results, and it caught many an unwary witness on the hop.

Leaving Constable Proudfoot to await the arrival

of a scenes-of-crime team, Falconer pointed himself towards the village pub. It was as good a place as any to start, and it was nearly lunchtime. The church clock was just striking twelve and George Covington was drawing the bolts on the front entrance to the pub as they approached it. Not being a town pub, it was not open all day.

The positioning of The Fisherman's Flies was ideal, for its south-facing garden allowed maximum enjoyment of the sunshine for those who felt so inclined, its north-facing bar was a haven of coolness in summer, and a log-fire-heated snug was exactly that in the winter months. Stepping in from the fierce midday July heat was like suddenly finding yourself underwater, and both policemen gave an involuntary shiver at the contrast in temperatures. Clematis, ivy and other vigorous climbing plants partly covered the pub's windows in their scramble upwards, making the lighting in the bar dim and green-tinged, re-enforcing the sub-marine atmosphere.

Ever-observant, Falconer had made a mental note of the licensee's name above the door, assumed it was he who would take responsibility for opening up, and thus addressed the man now behind the bar by name. 'Good day to you, Mr Covington. We'll take a little refreshment if we may, and then, perhaps, we could have a little chat.'

George Covington treated the introductions that followed with due solemnity, recommended the local smoked trout salad, and assured them that he and his wife would speak to them as soon as they had eaten.

After their excellent salad (although Carmichael

could not see what was wrong with a good steak and kidney pie, mushy peas, and chips with curry gravy), the landlord and his wife arrived together at their table, for although the tables at the front of the pub had filled rapidly, they had filled with the curious rather than the hungry. These 'customers' were more concerned with having a ringside seat for the unfolding village drama than with parting with any significant sums of money to maintain their places. They preferred to keep their money in their pockets, and their wits about them, in case they missed anything.

George and Paula Covington appeared an ill-matched couple when seen together. He seemed a typical country fellow in his late fifties. Broad, balding, and ruddy-complexioned, he was slow of movement, quietly spoken, and had surprisingly large hands and gentle grey eyes. His wife was the chalk to his cheese. She was about a decade younger, although her age was difficult to determine due to the amount of 'help' that she gave her appearance. Her hair was abundant and hennaed, her make-up heavy. Her proportions were generous and enhanced by a low-cut, close-fitting, leopard-patterned top and a short, narrow black skirt. She wore black stiletto-heeled shoes and a multiplicity of jangling gilt jewellery. Her voice, when she spoke, was slightly husky, probably from the cigarettes that she appeared to chain-smoke, and belied her London origins. She also displayed an unfortunate tendency to giggle in a flirtatious manner when spoken to by anyone of the opposite sex.

''E didn't come in more 'n once a week,' George

explained, when asked about Reg Morley's habits, 'and then 'e'd only 'ave an 'alf – made that last a two-hour stretch if 'e could. Tight-fisted old sinner 'e were, but not above cadgin' a drink off of anyone daft enough to put their 'and in their pocket. But 'e weren't no trouble. Sat by the fire in winter to save on 'eatin', same as a lot of old folk on a pension. 'Alf of mild's a lot cheaper than a scuttleful of coal.

'That little dog of 'is is a rare 'un, though, when it comes to beggin' for crisps and peanuts. Reg'lar card is that Buster, although Reg weren't above showin' 'im the boot when the mood was on 'im. Wonder what'll 'appen to 'im now.' (Falconer wondered what exactly had happened to him, as there had been no sign of a dog when they were at the cottage, and made a mental note to nip back and have a word with Proudfoot.) 'But no,' concluded the publican, 'Reg knew better than to cause trouble in 'ere.'

'But what about that slangin' match wiv the Brigadier?' his wife interrupted, a slight tartness in her tone indicating that she was feeling a little left out of the limelight. 'I thought the two old boys were goin' to come to blows, fists up, circlin' round they were, blowin' off enough 'ot air to fill a balloon.'

'When was this?' Falconer's interest had been diverted and he nodded to Carmichael to make sure that he was taking note of this.

'Friday night last,' George took over the narrative. 'Ol' Reg, 'e was sittin' beside the 'arth as usual, it bein' a breezy day, suppin' 'is 'alf, little Buster asleep under 'is chair, when in comes the

45

Brigadier an' 'is wife for a pink gin or three. Reg'lar as clockwork, those two are, on a Friday, seven-thirty on the dot. Well, we was fair busy with some summer folk who'd been up at the ruins and the trout farm – been 'avin' a look at the church, that kind of thing. Then about nine, it all thins out.'

'The Brigadier'd 'ad a few by then,' Paula interjected, eager to cut to the chase. ''E was soundin' off to the vicar and 'is wife about someone thievin'. Louder and louder 'e got, about someone raidin' 'is fruit an' veg patch, someone who'd 'ad 'is eggs and, maybe, even made off with a hen or two. Right purple in the face 'e was, an' then 'e spotted the old man over by the fireside, an' I thought 'is 'ead was goin' to explode, 'is face got so black.'

'I don't think it was quite that dramatic, Paula love.'

'It was indeed, George Covington,' she countered. 'Surely you recall 'ow 'e marched over an' 'auled 'im to 'is feet and barked into the old man's face that 'e deserved 'orsewhippin'?'

'Is that correct, Mr Covington?' Falconer cut in. There was a brief nod from the publican before his wife, the bit between her teeth now, galloped on with her narrative.

'And the old boy asked 'im what 'e was bellowin' about, and then 'e gave a sly sort of grin an' said that some folks 'ad so much it was amazin' as 'ow they 'ad the memory to miss a tiny morsel. Well, that was it, wasn't it? The Brigadier rolled up 'is sleeves, the two o' them raised their fists and began to circle. Pathetic, it was really, two men o' their age tryin' to act like they was twenty again.'

'That's when I went over and intervened, Inspector.' George took over the tale again. 'It wasn't as if I was worried about any damage. It was more the injured dignity I could see a-comin' that worried me. They'd made fools enough of themselves, and it was well-nigh time someone stopped them goin' any further.' This simple statement of fact showed the sturdy logic of George Covington's mind, an admirable character trait in a publican.

'And then what happened?'

'Nothin'. That were it.'

'Not quite, George, an' you know it. It was the language, Inspector. You should've 'eard it. Like when I was a nipper in the East End.' Paula Covington's eyes grew misty as she remembered more exciting times in her youth. She was grateful to have met George, and happy that he had asked her to be his wife. He was no oil-painting, but she had been well past her sell-by date when they had met, having had more than her fair share of fast-living when she was young, and, if her life was more sedate now, at least it was secure. George had taken her at face value and loved her for what she was. He thought himself a very lucky man to have her as his wife, and she, in her turn, was treated like a rare jewel.

Returning to the present, she continued, 'Fair effin' an' blindin' they were, old Reg callin' the Brigadier every name under the sun, the Brigadier threatenin' to set the dogs on 'im if ever 'e caught 'im on 'is property. Said 'e'd whip 'im to within an inch of 'is miserable, thievin' life if he tried anything like that again. 'Aven't 'eard language like

47

that since those sheep got loose and got into the caravan park,' she concluded with a sigh of nostalgia.

'It were all 'ot air, though,' George was quick to add. 'Eighty-three bells I counted this mornin' for old Reg, and the Brigadier's seventy-five if 'e's a day. Neither of 'em 'd've 'ad the strength to knock the skin off of a rice puddin' if you ask me.'

There being nothing of interest from that previous evening that either of them had heard or observed on the other side of the green, Falconer thanked them for their time and made preparations to leave.

IV

Outside it was the hottest part of the day, and the village shimmered in the unrelenting heat. Fewer newshounds dotted the green, and the ducks remained amongst the reeds or clustered under the shade of the trees, ready to take cover, should there be another barrage of stale bread and cake. Falconer decided to shelve the matter of the missing dog for the present. They would tackle the finder of the body first and, as they headed towards the post office, a lone wolf-whistle reminded him that Acting DS Jean-Paul Gaultier was as conspicuous as ever.

The post office was still closed for business, although whether for the lunch break or for the whole day was not indicated, so Falconer rang the bell for the private accommodation. Although his summons was answered in less than a minute, he could feel the perspiration begin to trickle down his back, and smell the dusty scent of the parched pavement as the door opened.

They were summoned inside by a whey-faced man, only a few years short of retirement, who looked like he carried the weight of the world on his shoulders. After introductions were effected he said, 'Do come in. We'll go upstairs to the sitting room, but would you mind being quiet. My wife's in bed with a migraine – she's a martyr to them – and I'd like her to sleep for as long as she can.' This request over, he walked slowly and quietly before them and showed them into a cool, shady room at the rear of the property that overlooked a pretty walled garden that must adjoin Crabapple Cottage.

The room was papered in a pale apricot sprigged with tiny daisies, the furniture was of oak, and chintz-upholstered. On the mantelpiece were several silver-framed photographs of a pretty girl, from baby to young woman, a wedding photograph, and one of the woman with two very young children, obviously the most recent.

'Our goddaughter and her family,' explained Alan Warren-Browne, seeing the direction of the inspector's glance. 'Do take a seat. I'm sure you'd like me to tell you what happened this morning.' And this he did, starting with the dog's barking, his wife's headache, and the unpleasant surprise awaiting him outside the post office door.

'I was pretty furious, I can tell you, and I banged like fury on his front door.' A little of the pallor left the postmaster's face as he remembered the intensity of his emotion. 'I felt like throttling the old devil. Oh, not literally,' he back-pedalled, recalling the circumstances, 'but I was so steamed up. I marched round to the back door, certain that he was hiding from me and laughing up his sleeve. I knew he was in there because of the dog, you see. He never went anywhere without Buster. I thought he wasn't answering the door on purpose.

'Anyway, I hammered on the back door a couple of times and shouted, then I tried the door handle and it wasn't locked. I fairly fell through it, the dog yelped and shot out, nearly having me over, then I saw him in the chair.'

'Did you touch anything, Mr Warren-Browne?' Might as well see if he would admit to any finger-prints that might be found, thought Falconer.

'Apart from the door, I think I put my hand on the wooden chair arm when I was checking that he wasn't unconscious or asleep, although only the dead could have slept through the racket that Buster had been making. But then, of course, he *was* dead.' The narrative dwindled to a halt. Acting DS Carmichael was sitting slightly out of the elderly man's eye-line, notebook open, tongue protruding from the side of his mouth in concentration, grateful for the momentary silence as he struggled to keep up with the narrative.

'And what did you do next?'

'Oh, I bolted. Couldn't get out of there fast enough. I was so panicked that I didn't even go back out the kitchen door. I blundered through the hall, had a beastly wrestle with the front door...'

'It was locked?' Falconer liked his detail as fresh as possible.

50

'It was, but the door had also dropped on its hinges, and when I unlocked it I had to give it a good heave to get out. There's probably a knack to it, but I didn't have time to think about that. Then I caught sight of Mrs Rollason from the teashop. I didn't want to disturb Marian any more, as she already had one of her beastly heads,' (here Falconer had to repress a smile at the mental image that this last phrase conjured up), 'so I called to Mrs Rollason to dial 999, then I'm afraid I closed up shop and went to bed. Felt absolutely washed out. Wife had taken a sleeping tablet and was already out of it. Felt I could do worse than join her.'

'And did you hear or see anything of Mr Morley yesterday, particularly during the evening? Anything, no matter how trivial it might seem to you, might put us on to someone who might have vital evidence.' Falconer's hunch muscle was telling him to become persuasive. After all, these people had been right next door when the deed had been done.

Much to his surprise (and annoyance) a voice from the door interrupted the flow. 'What's going on, Alan? Who are these gentlemen?'

In the doorway stood the slight, frail figure of Marian Warren-Browne, wrapped in a floral robe of some light material, a puzzled frown on her face.

'They're policemen, my dear.'

'Why, what's happened? It's not something to do with Kerry and the kiddies, is it?'

'No, nothing to do with them at all.'

'That beastly old man hasn't been making trouble again, has he?'

51

'Who's Kerry?' Falconer fired off simultaneously.

'Our goddaughter, Kerry Long. And no, only in so much as he's gone and got himself murdered,' replied Alan Warren-Browne, trying to answer both queries at the same time.

'What's your goddaughter got to do with the deceased?'

'What are you talking about, murdered?'

Falconer held up a hand and rose, calling for order and, when Marian had been apprised of the morning's events missed in her drug-induced sleep, returned to his own unanswered question. 'What has your goddaughter got to do with the deceased?' As he asked it, he could not prevent his eyes from straying to the photographs on the mantelpiece.

Marian Warren-Browne had slumped into one of the chintz-covered armchairs, and made no effort to speak. Her husband, ever protective, moved to fill the silence. 'Kerry lives in Jasmine Cottage, next door to Crabapple Cottage, and has been there since just after her marriage broke up. In fact, we secured the cottage for her so that we could help out with babysitting and suchlike.'

'More's the pity, the trouble it's caused the poor dear, living next to that monster.' Marian Warren-Browne lapsed back into silence again after this brief rally, laid her head back against the embroidered antimacassar and closed her eyes. Her skin looked grey in the north light from the sash window.

'That wicked old man has had it in for her since the day she moved in.' Alan Warren-Browne continued the explanation. 'The fact is, he just doesn't – sorry, didn't – like children. Made her life a misery over them playing and laughing, and then let that dog of his bark when he knew they were asleep, and let him get through the hedge and do his business in their garden. That's downright dangerous – a positive health hazard – with young children around.' He ground to a halt and looked across at his wife as if seeking guidance, but she was still sunk in post-migraine misery and did not notice his look.

With an expression of resolution on his face he continued, 'Anyway, there was something yesterday evening that I suppose you ought to hear about from us.' Marian's head began to rise. 'We'd been outside all afternoon, and it was getting on.'

'What time yesterday evening?' Falconer interrupted him as he sensed a change in the atmosphere.

Marian was now fully alert and cut in urgently, 'No, no, you mean yesterday afternoon, darling. Really, you're getting so muddled of late, I despair of you.'

Alan Warren-Browne's forehead creased, then relaxed slightly as he agreed. 'Silly of me, of course. What time was it, sweetheart?' For some reason Marian Warren-Browne was definitely in the driving seat now.

'When that dreadful noise was coming from the garage, you remember? So we couldn't really hear very clearly.'

'Of course. My wife's spot on. Heard Kerry having a good old harangue, but no idea what it was all about. Might just have been her shouting at the kiddies, I suppose.'

This was an abrupt volte-face, from 'something they ought to know', to 'just shouting at the kiddies', and Alan Warren-Browne looked as if he had had only a brief and very recent glance at the script. Something was being concealed, and Falconer would find out what it was, either from them or from someone else, and he did not care which.

Chapter Four

Monday 13th July – early afternoon

I

Back out in the early afternoon sunshine, Falconer and Carmichael walked the few short yards from the post office to Crabapple Cottage, where they found Constable Proudfoot still on guard at the front door, his face crimson in the heat, perspiration dripping from his nose and chin.

'Scene-of-Crime people been?' enquired Falconer.

'Yes, sir. And the police surgeon. Search just completed. Just need your authority to seal it off now.'

'By the way. Was there a little dog here this morning when you arrived?'

'Indeed there was, sir. Yappy little thing it was too, but seemed friendly enough.'

'And where is that friendly little dog now, Constable Proudfoot. You seem to have omitted to inform me of its whereabouts.'

'Miss Cadogan took it, sir. Old schoolmistress from Sheepwash Lane. She were here first thing, harassing me to let her take it and collect its things. I didn't know what else to do with it, so I let it go with her,' he blustered.

'Put it in your report, Proudfoot,' sighed the inspector, scandalised at this lax attitude. 'By the way, you've had a quick scout around. Anything worthy of mention?'

'No signs of forced entry. No signs of any search being made by person or persons unknown. Key still on the inside of the back door. Oh, and about nine thousand pounds in a box under the bed, mostly in old fivers.'

'What?'

Proudfoot gave him a 'not my fault this time' look, and turned his gaze skywards to follow the lazy course of a pigeon towards the oak trees on the green.

II

Carmichael had the good sense to keep quiet, as they walked next door to Jasmine Cottage. As they approached it, a figure hurried up to it, handbag slung casually over one shoulder. Although recognisable as the subject of the photographs on her godparents' mantelpiece, there had obviously not been a recent addition to their collection. The bloom had gone from Kerry Long's skin, she was a little too thin, and her features had become sharp, her expression harder. Maybe this was a result of the harsh realities of the breakdown of her marriage and single-parenthood, or maybe it was from the strain of a protracted battle with her unpleasant elderly neighbour. Falconer did not know the answer to this, but he meant to find out.

'Mrs Long?' he enquired.

'Ms Long,' she corrected him. 'Who wants to know?'

'Inspector Falconer – and this is Acting DS Carmichael. It's about Mr Morley next door.'

'If you find out who did it, let me know so I can buy them a drink.'

'I beg your pardon?'

'Sorry. That wasn't a very nice thing to say, was it?'

'Can we have a word?' he asked.

'I was just on my way back for a few minutes' break: I work over in Allsorts. Left the kiddies over there for a few minutes, so I can catch my breath. The rush has calmed down a bit now, as you lot haven't carted anyone off in handcuffs. The Punch and Judy show loses its shine when the puppets don't perform,' and with this some-what enigmatic turn of phrase she held the door open for them to enter.

Although the cottage was the same age, size and design as its counterpart next door, it could not have been more dissimilar in its interior. Crab-apple Cottage had been dark, grimy, uncared for and neglected. The tiny front room in Jasmine Cottage, into which the young woman now con-ducted them, was bright and cheery with white

56

walls and woodwork. Sensible washable covers in a royal blue and jade zigzagged pattern on the two-seater settee and single armchair, and a vase of scarlet roses on the polished mantelshelf lifted the spirits; there were cream curtains at the tiny windows, and pale washable rugs on the uneven floor completed the picture of a well-cared for home.

Falconer nodded approvingly and Carmichael positively beamed. He could do with just such a little gem as this place when he was ready to spread his wings. Seeing their expressions of approval, their hostess asked, rather shyly as if expecting a rebuttal, if they would like to see the rest of the downstairs, and Carmichael's enthusiastic, 'Please,' brought a smile to her face that dispelled the hardness that had sat there at their arrival.

A second door off the hall led to a tiny dining room which overlooked the back garden. Here, a cheap, white plastic patio set had been transformed with a tablecloth tie-dyed in yellow, orange and red, the chairs draped with crimson cotton. The same colour hung at the windows, and the old floorboards were (with young children in the house) sensibly bare and well-polished. So bright were the colours that Carmichael blended in splendidly, and Falconer looked as if he had suddenly faded to monochrome in comparison.

Kerry Long nodded towards the dining set next to which Carmichael was standing and murmured, 'It's amazing what you can do with some jumble sale sheets and a bit of imagination,' leaving the policemen in some doubt as to whether it was her own homemaking, or the younger man's peacock appearance, to which she was referring. And with that ambiguous remark, she led them out to the tiny kitchen at the back of the cottage.

It, too, was immaculate, the cupboards home-made many years ago, but freshly painted in a vivid lime green. Falconer's eyes darted back and forth in search of something he could not find, but had expected to be there. At last he gave in and asked, 'Where's your washing machine?'

With a rueful smile the young woman replied, 'Haven't got one. Can't afford it.'

'But you've got kiddies.' Carmichael was full of concern. His mum could not manage without hers. It was in use every day, sometimes two or three times. 'And them covers on the suite, and the rugs and stuff. How do you manage?'

'I manage all right, thank you, DS...'

'Carmichael. Acting.'

'DS Carmichael Acting it is, then. Most stuff I can manage myself. I'm used to hard work. Really heavy stuff my auntie takes into the launderette in Carsfold for me. That helps a lot.'

Although Falconer was aware that he had veered the conversation in this direction, it was becoming a little too cosily domestic for his liking, and he cleared his throat in an effort to get everyone's attention back to the matter in hand. 'About Mr Morley?' he prompted.

'Oh, I'm sorry, Inspector. Go back through to the front room and take a seat, and I'll see if I can be of any help.'

Back in the front room, and back to the more serious business on which they had called, Falconer asked the inevitable question. 'How well did

58

you get on with Mr Morley, Ms Long?' although the answer was fairly obvious from what they had already gleaned at the Post Office, and the young woman's reaction when they had arrived.

A cloud crossed her face, and the former hardness returned as she answered, 'Not at all. We didn't get on at all. Anyone'll tell you, so I better had. We were at loggerheads, and have been since we moved in here.'

'Can you tell me why?'

'I wish I knew.' Carmichael discreetly opened his notebook and began to scribble. 'He's had it in for me and the kids from the day we got here. He just doesn't like kids. If they lark around and play indoors, he bangs – oh, that should be banged – the wall at them. If they played in the garden, he yelled for them to shut up. If I went out and left washing on the line, nine times out of ten, he'd have a bonfire. And if me and the kids were trying to get a bit of peace and quiet, or they were asleep, he'd let that blasted dog of his out and set it off yapping. He'd shut it out in the garden for hours in all weathers, even though the stupid thing adored him and that's more than any other living creature did.

'And he'd encourage it into our garden for a "dump" when I was out. He was really foul to us, and we'd done nothing to him except exist and move in here.'

'Your godparents mentioned an incident yesterday afternoon,' he offered, deciding to hold fire on his hunch and gain her confidence, rather than alienate her. Relaxed, she was more likely to let something slip.

59

'Oh, that. Yes. That filthy old man had been throwing dog shit at my clean sheets. It takes ages to wash them in the bath, and he'd scored a direct hit right in the middle of a white double. I could've killed him,' she stated baldly, apparently unaware of the significance of what she had said. 'I shouted like hell over the fence, but the old sod wouldn't come out, so I had another shout out of the window when he took that shite-hound of his out for a walk. I mean, that stuff can blind kids, and I hate having to keep them out of the garden till I've been over it with a fine tooth comb. I got him later on, though, out the back, and really laid into him.' She sighed deeply. 'On the whole I'm rather glad he's dead.'

Falconer put a mental tick beside the Warren-Brownes' pathetic attempt to deceive him, and was rather surprised that this young woman should be so open in her hostility to one so recently murdered. She was either very naïve or very cunning.

The inspector felt he now had a fair idea of the state of open warfare that had existed between these neighbours and, if he only felt a fleeting and guarded sympathy for this outwardly hard young woman, Carmichael had obviously seen a rather different side to her, if the expression on his face were a reflection of his feelings. He had sided totally with the hard-working underdog, and he surveyed her and her immaculate home with open admiration. (So much for impartiality, thought Falconer.) This admiration did not seem to be reciprocated however, as, whenever she felt herself unobserved, Kerry darted incredulous glances at Carmichael's polychromatic length, as if she had never seen such a vision. Falconer smiled, as he imagined her to be sizing him up mentally to use as raw material for re-upholstery.

Dragging his thoughts back to the here and now, he asked, 'Did you notice or hear if anyone called next door yesterday evening? This could be very important.'

'I did hear a banging on his door and some shouting a bit after nine, maybe later, but I was in the bath.' The tiniest of the three bedrooms upstairs had been converted to house more modern washing facilities than those provided by a tin bath hanging on a nail on the back wall. 'But by the time I got out the noise had stopped.'

'So you've no idea who it was? Man or woman?'

'Oh, I'm fairly sure it was Nick Rollason – his wife runs the teashop. At least, when I looked out of the upstairs window, it was him I saw crossing the green from this direction, and I hardly think he'd've been to the post office at that time of night.'

'Any impressions from what you saw?' Falconer probed with little hope.

'Only that he might have been in the pub beforehand. He wasn't walking terribly well. Looked like he'd had a few. But he'd certainly come from over this way, and there was nowhere else that he could have been coming from.'

Thanking her for her frankness and co-operation, the two men took their leave of her and went back outside, momentarily blinded by the contrast from the shady interior to dazzling sunshine.

'Brave girl, that,' commented Carmichael. 'Two kids to bring up on her own, neighbour from hell

61

to contend with, got a job to hold down, no washing machine, and the house is immaculate. Wonder what fool let that gem get away.'

Wondering what fool had let Carmichael loose in the casual wear section of Marks & Blunders, Falconer said, 'Come on Acting DS Smitten. Stop mooning over it and let's see what the spider at the hub of the web has to say.'

'Beg pardon, sir?'

'The village shop, Carmichael, where else? The centre of all gossip, the fount and repository of all wisdom and knowledge, the reference library of life.'

'Yes, sir.' Carmichael knew when he was out of his depth, but who the hell was this Smitten bloke when he was at home?

III

The village shop lived up to its name of 'Allsorts'. Dim and cool inside, it was like an Aladdin's cave of anything a rural dweller could want, without the inconvenience of a trip to town (with the exception of combine harvesters and livestock). A multiplicity of goods filled shelves, hung from the walls, and crouched on the floor, so many obstacles for the unwary or unobservant. Galvanised and plastic buckets jostled for place with mop-heads, old-fashioned Sunlight soap (do they still make that? wondered Falconer, disbelieving the evidence of his own eyes), clothes pegs and kindling. Bottles and jars, packets and boxes filled the central counter, alongside an array of cleaning materials, dishcloths and dusters. The far wall housed a refrigeration unit and a freezer: the main counter and till were surrounded by newspapers, magazines, greeting cards, sweets and tobacco products.

Behind this counter was a round, rubber ball of a woman, overweight in a not-unattractive way. Probably in her mid-fifties, her grey hair was permed and immaculate, her overall clean and fresh, her smile genuine. 'How can I help you gentlemen?' she enquired, her voice belying her northern roots.

Falconer held out his warrant card and made the necessary introductions.

'It's about old Morley you'll be wanting to know,' she surmised, holding out her hand. 'I'm Rosemary Wilson – Mrs. I'm the owner.'

'That's right, Mrs Wilson. We're just trying to get a general picture of what the unfortunate gentleman was like, see if we can't clear up this sorry business as quickly as possible. We thought that, as the shop was probably the central meeting point for the village, you might be in a position to give us a few pointers.' Falconer was not above flattery in his quest for information.

'I don't like to gossip.' Fifteen-love to Mrs Wilson. He had made an error of judgement.

'I'm sure you don't, Mrs Wilson. I just thought that you might be able to give us a character sketch of him as a customer.' The inspector was back-pedalling now, but it seemed to have worked.

'I do know he was a fair old nuisance to many. Never a pleasant word to say about anyone, and many an unpleasant one to folk's faces, as well as behind their backs, in the hope they'd get to hear

63

about it.'

'Is there anyone in particular you feel you can tell us about,' he probed, aware that this was just the start of the investigation and, should it prove to be a non-straightforward one, he would need the trust of as many of the villagers as he could get.

'I really don't want to speak out of turn, Inspector.'

'Anything at all would be helpful, Mrs Wilson.' Really, thought Falconer, this was not at all how he had envisaged this conversation. He should now be overwhelmed with a torrent of local rumour, malice and spite. This was more like pulling teeth.

'Well,' she capitulated slightly, 'he didn't like the Warren-Brownes at the post office. He had them down as stuck-up because of their double-barrelled name, and them liking to keep themselves to themselves. He had it in for them.'

'In what way did he have it in for them? Can you be a bit more specific?' Falconer knew he was covering old ground here, but encouraged the woman, to check the accuracy of what he had already been told. If her account tallied with the one the Warren-Brownes had offered, it meant that any further information from this source could probably be relied upon.

'Well, Mrs Warren-Browne – Marian – is an absolute martyr to them migraine headaches – these painkillers here,' she pointed to her right on the display behind her, 'I started stocking just for her. Now, not even they are strong enough, and the doctor's trying to find something as'll work for her. And Mr Warren-Browne – Alan – he's

64

that protective of her, her being so frail.'

'And Mr Morley?' prompted the inspector, aware of time passing. Carmichael, sensing repetition, had lost all interest in the proceedings and was gawping round the wares displayed with keen interest.

'He goaded that dog of his,' she continued. 'Goaded it, every opportunity he got, to make it bark. Knew it would set her off with one of her heads.' Once more Falconer could not afford the luxury of time to enjoy this vision. He would have to save that for later. 'And the old man seemed to time his dog's walks so that it would quite often do its business outside the post office. Can't blame the animal, of course, and Reg Morley wouldn't know a poop scoop if one hit him in the eye.' (Another surreal vision for later.) Mrs Wilson's questing finger to the wall on her left, indicated a multicoloured array of what were described on the backing cardboard as 'Doggy-Do-Aways'.

'Anything else you feel able to help us with?' the inspector interjected at this natural break.

'Bit of a dirty old man, as well,' she offered.

'How did that manifest itself?' he prompted her, elbowing Carmichael in the ribs, to rouse him to take note of this new information.

'Why do you think he walked that dog of his in the woods? Young courting couples, of course! Dirty old man! Better than the telly, he thought, if he could have a good peek at young folks' goings-on.' The shopkeeper finished with a snort of disgust and a moue of distaste.

'What about relations with his other neighbours?'

This seemingly innocent question must have touched a nerve, for she coloured momentarily and said, 'If you really want to know about him why don't you speak to his nephew – or rather, great-nephew, I should say. He'll give you chapter and verse, I don't doubt. His name's Mike Lowry and he runs the garage – out of the shop and it's opposite on your right.' And more than this she refused to say.

As they exited, Carmichael summed up his impressions of the shop. 'Funny smell in there, and it seemed so old-fashioned, it ought to have been in black and white.'

Unlike you, my lad. Unlike you! Falconer could not suppress the thought.

IV

Castle Farthing Garage was just in Drovers Lane, which ran west from the village green. It had a small forecourt with three petrol pumps, a small pre-fabricated shop that sold only car-related products, and a workshop at the rear where repairs and MOTs were carried out. The pumps were not self-service, and an oil-smeared notice on the shop door directed any callers to the workshop.

It was here that Falconer and Carmichael found the proprietor, his oil-stained overall legs pro-truding from under an elderly Mini. By the side of the car a transistor radio blared, and it was only by directing Carmichael to switch this off (Falconer did not want to get oil on his hands) that the inspector gained the mechanic's attention.

As he rose from his prone position, the begrimed young man caught sight of Carmichael and let out a hoot of amusement. 'I hope you won first prize.' He grinned. 'You certainly worked hard on your costume.' This comment drew a blush from the young policeman and a frown of disapproval in his direction from his superior. He really would have to speak to Carmichael about his plain clothes being a little more, well, *plain*, in the future.

Lowry did not deny his blood-tie with the old man, but said there had been a family rift, years before he was born, between his great-uncle Reg and the rest of the family, and he had hardly ever spoken to the old man, as he did not seem of a mind to let bygones be bygones. 'I never did have any idea what the original tiff was about – blew up over something and nothing, I seem to recollect, the way a lot of these things do. He were a right hard old sinner, though, and visited his contempt down the generations,' he explained, wiping his hands on a rag so oily it was probably achieving the opposite of his intentions.

'So you had little to do with him?'

'Best part of nothing. He wouldn't acknowledge my existence: I didn't want to know him.'

'Were you working here yesterday evening, Mr Lowry? Did you happen to notice anyone cross that way towards Mr Morley's cottage?'

Lowry shook his head. 'I was closed up out front and working out here under this little wreck. Not sure what time I finished. I was that beat, I washed up and went straight to bed.'

'And you live where?'

'Here. Back of the shop. Sort of bed-sit, but it

67

does me.'

Mike Lowry was a slimly built man, tall and rangy, with fair hair and grey eyes that never wavered from the face of the person to whom he was speaking. He had a certain charisma that even Falconer, as a male, could recognise (and resent), and he put the question that this, together with the last bit of information, left uppermost in his mind. 'Not married then, Mr Lowry?'

'Was.' The muscles in Lowry's face tautened, and Falconer found himself probing deeper – but, hell, he wasn't being nosy, it was his job to ask questions.

'Anyone local?'

'Yes.'

'Name?'

'Any of your business?'

'Might be. Now, what's the missus's name. I'm sure there are plenty who would be willing to tell me.'

'Kerry.'

'Not Kerry Long?'

'Went back to her maiden name.'

Falconer suddenly felt a penny drop. 'So those children next door were actually Reg Morley's own flesh and blood. Well, I'll be damned. And you say you had no occasion to speak to him, not even about how he was treating her and the children?'

'She had no need of me to defend her.' Lowry was beginning to look aggressive. 'Not with that Auntie Rosemary of hers, riding into battle for her.'

A further penny began to roll towards the edge.

68

'That wouldn't be Auntie Rosemary Wilson, by any chance?'

'Got it in one, Sherlock! She's like Boadicea when she's roused, believe you me. I've had the rough side of her tongue on more than one occasion, and it's left me reeling.'

Falconer was still puzzled. Village ways were a closed book to him and he sought enlightenment. 'Ms Long said nothing about having been married to you, or your relationship to Mr Morley, and neither she nor Mrs Wilson said anything about being related to each other. How do you explain that, man?' he asked in exasperation.

Lowry stared at him as if he was stupid. 'You probably didn't ask them.'

Chapter Five

Monday 13th July – afternoon

I

At the vicarage in Church Lane, Bertie Swainton-Smythe was in his study, working on his sermon for the following Sunday, but apart from a facetious phrase in Hebrew and the words 'Pentecost 6' at the top of the sheet, the paper remained stubbornly blank. His wife Lillian was vigorously dusting the numerous bookshelves that lined the walls. What light managed to penetrate this gloomy sanctuary merely highlighted its shabbiness. The carpet was worn through to its backing in places, the curtains frayed, the furnishings not so much antique as 'early jumble sale'. Chipped and battered ornaments spoke of a boisterous brood of children, but no such brood had ever blessed their union.

'I don't know why you're letting the death of that old goat get to you, Bertie. He was hardly a Christian soul, rarely in church. Not what you'd call a regular worshipper, and when he was there you know he helped himself from the collection, rather than part with a penny to add to it. In fact you said yourself that he only came to services when he was short of a bob or two.'

'Suspected, Lillian, suspected. I never had any proof, and I never confronted him,' chided the Reverend Bertie, somewhat hurt by his wife's forthright manner.

'Suspected, be blowed. Don't be such an old hypocrite,' accused Lillian, pulling out an ancient set of bound eighteenth-century sermons by some obscure country cleric, in pursuit of a spider. 'You said yourself that takings were always down when he turned up.' A muffled thump and a grunt of satisfaction showed that she had achieved her objective.

'Why, at Easter, the Brigadier said that when you cashed up,' (her husband winced at such a commercial description), 'that he had put a ten-pound note in the bag, and there wasn't a sign of it, and no one has admitted to the twenty drachma coin that was in there, either. What other conclusion is there to draw?'

'One mustn't condemn without proof, my dear.

And if the old man's needs were greater than God's, who are we to stand in judgement?'

'Oh, stop being such a saint, Bertie. Wake up and smell the coffee. Don't you remember the uproar he caused when you wanted to move the time of the carol service last year, so that the kiddies could join in and do a little nativity scene? I honestly thought there'd be blood on the pews before he was over-ruled. Really, some of the old folk in this parish seemed to be as anti-kiddie as he was. At times, I could hardly believe the evidence of my own ears.'

At this, the vicar put down his pen and squared himself up for confrontation. 'A little eccentric he may have been, but I will not have ill spoken of the dead in my own study, in my own vicarage, by my own wife.'

'Bertie, you said you could have throttled him, when he said that children shouldn't be allowed to have anything to do with Christmas.'

'Figure of speech.'

'And that they should be seen and not heard, and how they'd all turn out better if they were locked in an understairs cupboard for cheeking their elders and betters.'

'That is enough, Lillian. He was an old man and he has been murdered. He's been murdered in my parish, and I won't sit here and stand for it,' he concluded in somewhat muddled terms. 'I simply won't stand for it.'

And he did not have to for, at that moment, the front doorbell wheezed asthmatically through the first half of the main theme of that infernal piece by Beethoven ('Ode to Joy'), and faltered to a flat-

71

battered halt, as Bertie tugged on the ill-fitting lump of wood that was the vicarage door. The vicarage faced north, and the aforementioned door was a martyr to the weather, never quite making up its mind whether to shrink and admit shrieking draughts, or swell and try the patience of a near-saint. Whichever it chose made little difference to this hypochondriac piece of carpentry, so long as it drew attention to itself.

'Must get this seen to,' he puffed, as he revealed Falconer and Carmichael waiting impatiently on the step. 'Ah, we meet again.'

'Indeed we do,' concurred Falconer, cocking a sardonic eyebrow. 'If you can spare us the time, we need to go through exactly what happened earlier on today, and then see if there's any other information you may have to offer us, that might prove useful in the course of this investigation.'

Bertie looked pained. 'I don't know that I know anything helpful.'

'Ah, you'd be surprised at how much you do know, Reverend, and how useful even the most trivial of things might prove.'

At this moment the door from the study opened, and the gap left by it was partly breached by a stout figure holding a feather duster. 'Friends of yours, Bertie? Hadn't you better make some introductions before I begin to feel left out? Just got back from your holidays, son?' this last to Carmichael as her gaze travelled down his Technicolor length. Her voice was husky, with a persuasive quality that left the listener anxious to please.

'Of course, my dear. This is my wife Lillian. Lillian, this is Mr Falconer – Inspector, if I remember right.' Bertie indicated the shorter of the two callers, beaming at his feat of memory, then his face clouded as he surveyed the rainbow-clad Everest that was caller number two. 'I'm afraid I seem to have forgotten the name of your, ah, multi-coloured colleague,' he admitted, a wave of crimson washing up from beneath his clerical collar, lest his description cause offence.

'Carmichael, Vicar. Davey Carmichael,' carolled the young giant, not in the least offended.

As they followed the incumbent and his wife down the narrow, gloomy corridor in search of the sitting room, Falconer looked puzzled. He had had a quick look at Carmichael's file (no questions asked) when they had been thrown together, as it were, and this did not tally. 'I thought your name was Ralph.'

''Tis.'

'Then why did you say you were called Davey?'

''Cos I am.'

'Let me get this right, your name's Ralph, but you're called Davey?'

'Yes.'

'Is Davey your middle name?' All this sotto voce as they walked.

'No.'

'David?'

'No.'

'Then why?' Falconer pleaded for enlightenment in an exasperated whisper.

'If you had a name like Ralph, wouldn't you prefer to be called Davey, or something else ordinary?'

'Don't you have a middle name you could use?'

73

'Yes. But I don't want to.'

'What is it?'

'Not telling.'

'That's an order, Carmichael.'

'Orsino. Me mum saw some play when she were having me and liked the sound of it.'

''Nuff said.' Harry Falconer could not see too much wrong with the name Ralph, but anyone whose mother had saddled her son with a name like Orsino deserved at least a little sympathy and tact.

II

The reception room referred to as the 'sitting room' proved as unwelcoming as Falconer had imagined, from his first impressions of the vicarage. A selection of misfit chairs and a sofa, all dating from the three immediate post-war decades, clung to the walls like maidens shunning the dance. No two pieces shared the same upholstery, and the carpet was a much-worn nylon twist in a nauseous shade of mustard. In the centre of the room stood a coffee table that had obviously achieved its current status by the use of a saw (not quite evenly) on the legs of, what had once been a hall or small dining table. A bulky television set with enough dials and knobs to declare it pre-remote control lurked in a corner, and the windows were framed with slightly too short, dull gold-coloured curtains in unlined brushed nylon. This room faced east and north and had little light at this time of the afternoon.

Bertie Swainton-Smythe confirmed to the two policemen how he had heard of the death of one of his parishioners, and how he had reacted to this news, describing his earlier meeting with the inspector in the kitchen of Crabapple Cottage, and of course his visit to St Cuthbert's to pray for Reg Morley's immortal soul.

At the conclusion of his narrative, Lillian shooed him off to make coffee, as she obviously had some business of her own to conduct. Her eager flow of gossip merely confirmed the relationships between the deceased, his neighbours and his great-nephew, but when the monologue (with breaks for suitable exclamations) reached the village shop, she did have something new to impart.

'...and it wasn't just his treatment of Kerry and the children, even though Mrs Wilson feared the boys getting toxocara from the dog's mess. He was a thieving old git.' Both policemen looked mildly disapproving of such uncharitable language from the wife of a man of the cloth. 'And don't you cock your eyebrows at me. You didn't know him. He'd pocket anything he could. She had to watch him like a hawk, once she'd found out who was respon-sible for the bulk of her shrinkage – that doesn't sound right, but you know what I mean.' Car-michael grunted as his pen flew across the page of his notebook, in an effort to keep up with the flow, Falconer nodded, not wishing to speak and stem it.

'And do you remember Easter this year?' she called in the direction of the kitchen. 'It was that wet, I told Auntie I'd have to order some cubits of wood, so that Bertie could get on with building an ark. Anyway, that week when it rained pretty much non-stop was the week that Mrs Wilson went up north to visit her family, and she left a friend of hers from Carsfold in charge of the shop.

'Well, that Reg Morley could sniff out a 'live one' at a hundred paces. When he worked out he wasn't being watched like a hawk, he starts to ingratiate himself with the temporary help when Kerry was on her breaks. The help was a fairly old dear herself, and by the time Mrs Wilson gets back from her little trip, he's run up a slate into three figures, and got the old dear to keep it to herself and not bother Kerry with the details.

'Try as she might, I don't think Rosemary's seen a penny back this four-month. Maybe now he's dead, she'll be able to make a claim against his estate. I know she could do with it. That little shop's been that close to closing down many a time, and something like this could be the straw that breaks the camel's back.'

'Not gossiping, I hope, dear?' asked the Reverend Bertie, returning with a laden tray.

'Of course not, Pops.'

Short for 'Sweetie Pops'? wondered Falconer, who, not being a sentimental man, shuddered, mentally searching for a new direction for the conversation and unexpectedly finding it in Carmichael.

'What about the little dog in all this? His owner's dead, but we've not seen him. All we know is that someone came and took him away...' He faltered to a halt, slightly embarrassed at being the centre of attention, and Bertie's next remark did not help.

'What a kind-hearted young man you are. No,

76

I'm glad to say that poor Buster has been taken in by a kind neighbour with an excellent pedigree. In fact, she's my wife's aunt. Martha Cadogan.'

'The old schoolmistress?'

'That's right.' Lillian took the conversational reins. 'Auntie and Reg Morley were of an age, at school together, knew each other all their lives, although not intimately as friends. She persuaded that rather crimson constable to let her have Buster's bits and pieces, and took the little animal off to her place, saying that, even if he only stayed for a while, he'd be company, and the extra exercise would be good for her arthritis.'

'Aunt Martha is an angel.'

'I wouldn't go that far, Bertie, but her heart's in the right place, and if someone hadn't taken responsibility, that dog would have been a real nuisance running loose.'

'So your aunt must have known quite a bit about Mr Morley over the years?' prompted the inspector.

'She'd known him as long as anyone locally, and probably as well,' agreed Lillian.

'And where does she live?' Proudfoot had mentioned where, but they had not made a note of it at the time.

'Right up the High Street, turn left into Sheepwash Lane, third property on the left – The Old School House, it's called.'

III

Upon leaving the vicarage, Falconer and Carmichael returned to Crabapple Cottage to give it the once-over, now that forensic evidence had been taken and the body removed. Proudfoot had shown them the battered box of crumpled and ancient grubby bank notes, and had been dismissed with it, to lodge it at headquarters in Market Darley for safekeeping.

Looking round them now, even with the addition of fingerprint powder, the place seemed no more grubby, and they commenced their search, Falconer with a handkerchief fastidiously wrapped round his right hand.

In the kitchen-cum-scullery they found little more than cracked and chipped crockery, elderly cooking pots and half-used packets and jars of various foodstuffs. There was no refrigerator, and foods liable to spoil were kept in an old-fashioned metal meat safe, on a slab of marble in the larder. It was Falconer who made this discovery, and he immediately instructed Carmichael to dispose of the contents with some haste. The milk had turned in the heat, and the few rashers of bacon in there seemed intent on following it. Falconer's face was a picture of disgust as he withdrew from the claustrophobic space, a hand over his mouth and nose.

A plethora of bills, both paid and unpaid, resided behind the mantel clock, and the two drawers by the sink held a collection of unmatched cutlery, and several money-off coupons for such items as dog food and tea bags. The sink itself held two or three inches of greasy water and several unwashed items, including a saucepan, probably the one used to heat the milk for the old man's cocoa.

78

The middle room was empty except for a battered table, a wooden chair, a lop-sided stool, and several teetering piles of books which proved all to have come from the County Library, and which should have been returned, some as long as twenty-three years ago. So the old man had had a hobby after all, and it seemed to be kleptomania.

The tiny front room had little to yield in the way of information on first inspection, but presented plenty for them to sift through. Newspapers were ranged in piles around the walls, as if the old man had never thrown anything away. One armchair was piled high with an assortment of broken clocks and radios, and an old bureau seethed with a collection of paperwork that probably stretched back over several decades. The one electric light hung, unshaded, from the centre of the ceiling. There was no television set.

After some time, Falconer suggested that they just bundle up the contents of the bureau, plus anything else that looked of interest, and take it all back to the station with them, so that they could examine it in more salubrious surroundings. This agreed, Carmichael was dispatched to the shop to purchase some black refuse sacks, while Falconer climbed the stairs to see if any clue awaited them there.

There were three rooms upstairs, none of which had been converted to a bathroom. Two of them were stacked with a variety of items: old bicycles, bits of what could once have been lawnmowers, wooden tennis racquets in old-fashioned presses, pictures with dilapidated frames and cracked glass, gloomy Victorian vases – a veritable Aladdin's cave of jumble. The third, and largest, room was obviously where the old man slept. It contained a huge and very ugly walnut-veneered wardrobe with matching monstrous dressing table, a marble-topped washstand (with period basin and ewer, and probably in use since the old man's childhood), and an iron-framed bed complete with greyish sheets, old army-surplus blankets and two un-slipped pillows, the whole in unmade disarray.

Under the bed where the cache of cash had been discovered there was also what is known in the vernacular as a 'gazunder'. Falconer pulled this out, then wished he had not, for it was un-emptied from the night before Reg Morley had met his maker, and was more than a little fragrant.

Wrinkling his nose with distaste, he made a hasty perusal of the contents of dressing table and wardrobe, and was just finishing when Carmichael returned. 'Right, I'll bag up that stuff, you deal with what's under the bed, my lad. I think you'll find there's a privy somewhere out the back.'

'Thanks, sir.'

'Don't mention it.'

He was just about to put the last of the papers into the black bag when Carmichael returned holding something very gingerly by its edge. 'What have you got there?'

'Don't know, sir. Seems like a funny coin thing, but it doesn't quite seem like proper money. I've never seen anything like it before.' Carmichael held out his discovery, which was about the size of an old half-crown, but rather heavier. A copper coin, it held an intricate pattern on one side, the date 1787 just discernible, and on the other, a worn profile of what appeared to be a male figure, hooded and with a beard. Any wording once engraved on its surfaces, bar the date, had long been worn to illegibility.

'What is it, sir?'

'I've no idea. Where did you find it?'

'Down the edge of the path next to the privy. It was only luck that I saw it.'

'It's probably been there for years. It's not exactly Ground Force out there. Give it here,' Falconer pocketed it, 'and I'll look it up when I get a minute, see if I can find out what it is.' And so saying, he gathered up the sack of papers, together with another small bag of assorted debris they had accumulated during their search. 'You lock up, Carmichael. I reckon we're about done here for today.'

IV

Outside once more, and away from the oppressive atmosphere of the cluttered little cottage, Falconer pulled his pocket watch from his waistcoat pocket (one of his little affectations, for he wore no wrist watch) and, after consulting it, decided, 'I think we'll call it a day for now. We'll start up at that old dear's tomorrow morning, then see who else there is to be seen, finish playing "Grass Thy Neighbour". Then we can consolidate and start on Round Two.' Round Two was Falconer's favourite part of an investigation. He always moved very softly in his initial enquiries while he gathered

81

ammunition. Round Two was ambush time.

As he dropped Carmichael off at his family home he ventured, 'Oh, and Carmichael – Davey – tomorrow, do you think you could...' but he was lost for words.

'I could what, sir?'

'You know, your dress.'

'What dress?'

'Your attire.'

'I'm a what?'

'Your garb.'

'Sorry, sir. You've lost me.'

'Wear darker colours, man. You look like a mobile paintbox.' There, he had said it. Exasperation had dragged it out of him, but that could not be all bad if it meant that they were not quite so conspicuous on the morrow.

'Sir?'

'Yes?'

'Forget the "Davey" bit. Carmichael'll do fine, if you don't mind.'

'Carmichael it is, then, er, Carmichael.' Touché!

Chapter Six

Tuesday 14th July – morning

I

Harry Falconer pulled up outside Victoria Terrace the following morning with a sick feeling of dread. He had already caught a glimpse of what lurked at the side of the porch. As the little sports car drew to a halt, what seemed to be an inordinately tall shadow detached itself from the property and advanced towards the waiting vehicle.

'Mornin', Sir.'

'Good morning, Carmichael.' The inspector's baleful gaze took in the sight of a six-and-a-half-foot mourner in search of a funeral. Carmichael had taken Falconer at his word, nay at more than his word, and divested his appearance of all trace of colour. Today he wore only black: black trainers and socks, black knee-length shorts and a black tee shirt (no motif). On his head sat a similarly plain black baseball cap, still worn the right way round. His eyes were hidden behind black-framed sunglasses. He looked, Falconer thought, not unlike the angel of death on his way to a disco.

'This dark enough for you, sir?' the younger man asked as he folded himself, like a human ironing board, into the passenger seat.

'You look like you're about to make me an offer on something in oak with brass handles.'

'Come again, sir?'

'Nah!' Falconer drove off, aware that his companion for today appeared to be an escapee from a Mafia picnic at the very least. Was there no happy medium for the lad?

II

Following the directions they had received the previous day, Falconer headed straight for Sheepwash Lane, to the left off the top end of the High Street, and found The Old School House with no difficulty. From its appearance, in the past this had obviously been the old Church of England village school, recognisable from the narrow, high-set, ecclesiastical windows visible to front and sides. The land to the front, and running part of the way down both sides, was tarmacked, and must have been the playground in its previous usage. They were unable to see round to the back of the property, as their view was obstructed by fencing smothered in a variety of climbing plants, the air thick with their scent.

The ringing of the front door bell produced a frenzied tirade of barks, and the door half-opened to reveal a white-haired, elderly woman holding on to the collar of a small dog, which she expertly fielded into a side room before opening the door full, and greeting her visitors with a broad smile.

'Mrs Cadogan?' began the inspector.

'Miss.'

'My apologies. Miss Cadogan. Detective Inspector Falconer and Acting DS Carmichael. May we have a few words with you, please?'

'If you show me your warrant cards.'

These produced, she took them, put the security chain on the door, and went in search of her reading glasses, leaving the two men on the step feeling a little foolish, and not much more than five years old. Returning a minute or two later, she unchained the door, handed back their IDs and bade them come in. Martha Cadogan was nobody's fool, and she took nothing at face value. As they entered, she eyed Carmichael up and down and asked, 'Have you recently suffered a loss, young man?'

She led them right through the house and into the back garden, where she shepherded them over to a wrought-iron garden table surrounded by four chairs. Returning briefly indoors, she re-emerged carrying two tumblers. On the table stood a half-empty (or half-full, depending on whether one is a pessimist or an optimist) tumbler and a jug full of ice-cubes and an opaque liquid. Small beads of moisture on the outside of the jug attested to the liquid's cooling properties.

'Home-made lemonade, gentlemen?' she offered, and had poured for them before they had time to answer. Lowering herself carefully into a cushioned chair, the little dog at her feet, she asked, 'How may I be of assistance? I presume you've called about yesterday's unpleasant discovery?'

It was obvious that she had been a schoolteacher. Carmichael had removed his baseball cap and was sitting to attention. Even Falconer looked like a man on his best behaviour. 'Is that Mr Morley's dog? I understood from your niece that you had rescued it,' Falconer enquired.

'I did indeed rescue it. And it's a he.' A glint of something as cold and hard as steel had appeared in her eyes. 'That wretched John Proudfoot was only going to pack him off to the RSPCA sanctuary. He even refused, at first, to let me in to feed him. Well, that's when a few home truths came in handy. Three years I taught him, on this very property, before his family moved to Carsfold. He needed reminding of the snotty-nosed little wretch who used to wet himself during story-time, rather than put up his hand to be excused.'

'And that worked, did it?' Falconer knew it had worked: knew it would have worked on him, too, and more effectively than any order from his senior officers in his army days. Carmichael merely looked intimidated and fingered the peak of his cap nervously.

'I'll say it did, young man. I had that poor dog and all his bits and pieces out of there in a trice. Unless, or until, someone claims him he'll be company for me, and walking him will give my old bones a good stretch. But was it just the dog you came to enquire about, Inspector?'

Pulling himself together, Falconer launched into coaxing-out whatever background information about the deceased, and his chequered relationships with the other villagers, that he could.

'A long time? I've known him all his life, young man. He was a nasty, spiteful little boy who grew into a nasty, spiteful old man. All his life he'd never do anyone a good turn if he could do them a bad one.' (Goodness, they called a spade a spade in Castle Farthing.)

'When we were at school, you had to keep your eye on anything you had – marbles, sweeties, comics – or he'd be away with them. And if we girls went out to the old earth closet, we went in twos, one to use it, the other to check round the back to see that little Reggie Morley wasn't on 'knickers-watch'. And I lost count of the little girls who went home in tears because he'd dipped their pigtails in the inkwell. He did it to me once, but only the once, mind. And he never changed.' She sighed, floating on a cloud of memory and lost youth.

'Can you recall anyone whose back he may have put up, recently, Miss Cadogan?' Falconer broke through her reverie.

'Oh, I can give you a list, but it's a long one,' and she enumerated the grievances with the Brigadier, with Mrs Wilson, Kerry Long, and Mike Lowry. Her final pieces of information were, however, news to them.

'I'm sure my niece mentioned all the bother he's caused at the church. Really, Bertie is a saint to have put up with a man who was hardly what one would call a regular worshipper.'

This was news indeed, and Falconer did not want to alert the lady to his total ignorance. 'Yes, if you'll just go through the main grievances for the sake of accuracy and verification,' he encouraged, hoping she would not see through his bluff. This was 'Grass Thy Neighbour' at its best.

87

'Lillian seemed to think he was light-fingered with the collection, but she had no definite proof. No, it was more the trouble he'd make whenever there was a special service, as if he wanted to blight it for everyone else.'

'What sort of trouble did he cause?'

'Usually just bad feeling, like when Bertie wanted to change the time of the carol service, but last harvest was rather more horrible.'

'Go on.'

'Well, there was some sort of to-do about what would go in the old folks' hampers – they're made up from the harvest offerings and go to old folk (like me, I suppose) in the village. Some of us, though, don't really need them, and thought it would be nice if some of the produce could go to the cottage hospital.'

'And Mr Morley didn't agree?' Falconer's voice was very quiet and controlled.

'He wasn't the only one, but he was the most abusive.'

'So what happened? What did he do?'

'No one knows for sure it was him, but when Bertie arrived for service on the morning of the harvest festival, all the fruit and vegetables had been cut up and mutilated, and weren't fit for anything but the pig bin.'

'Did Mr Morley, or anyone else, have access to a key?'

'Didn't need to. Bertie opens the church at seven-thirty for early communion, and he doesn't lock it between services, in case someone needs to look in for a prayer or solace.'

'Not very nice,' judged Falconer. 'Did he have

any other unpleasant traits?'

'Has anyone mentioned that he was a bit of a peeping tom?' A vision of the village shopkeeper arose in the inspector's mind as he confirmed that, yes, they had been told of the old man's proclivities. 'Well, beyond the garden wall here,' Miss Cadogan pointed, 'is an access road, little more than an alleyway that runs down from the end of the terrace of cottages in Drovers Lane, turns right, past the end of my garden, past next door, and ends with access to The Rookery and the teashop.'

'And?' Falconer resisted the temptation to ask where all this geography was leading.

'I know for sure that he's been spying on that young Rebecca Rollason – runs the teashop and lives next door at The Rookery.'

'You know for sure, or you've heard.'

'Oh, I know, young man. I was out putting my dustbin in the alley late one evening a week or so ago, and I heard a noise. When I went down to see what it was, Reg Morley pushed past me and nearly knocked me flat, in his haste to get away.'

'You're sure it was him?'

'My nose, alone, confirmed it,' she said rather tartly and with a sniff. 'And Buster was with him, so that was a bit of a give-away.'

'What did you do next?'

'I went down to see if I could see what he'd been up to. When I got to the end of the alley, the only light was coming from upstairs at The Rookery. The curtains weren't drawn and young Rebecca was just putting on her night-dress.'

This was shaping up nicely, as Nick Rollason

had (unconfirmed, but probable) called on Reg Morley on the night of his death. Falconer plunged in with a question. 'Did you tackle the old man about his behaviour?'

'There was no point. He'd been like that since childhood, as I told you. No, I went and had a quiet word with her husband when next I saw him, and suggested that drawing the curtains was probably a good idea.'

'Is that all then, Miss Cadogan?' Falconer was preparing to rise, nodding at Carmichael that the interview was at an end.

'Except for those other two, and I really don't know whether he knew anything about it, or even if I ought to mention it, as it doesn't yet seem to be common gossip.'

'What other two?' Falconer was right back down in his chair again, all ears.

'It's Mrs Romaine from next door and Mr Manningford from the corner house.'

'What about them?'

'I had better set the scene first. The Romaines have three children away at school. He works in Carsfold – he's a financial adviser, I think; he commutes – and she's a freelance artist – has a studio at the end of their garden. The Manningfords live next door. She's a bit older than him, one of those interior designers, works away a lot, no children. He works from home. Can you see what I'm leading up to, Inspector?'

'You'd better lead me there, Miss Cadogan.'

'She works from home: he works from home. The studio's well away from the house – an ideal place for a tryst. They seem to forget that I'm here during the day, even if everyone else within ear-shot is out at work. Sometimes I've had to go in from the garden. But it's not my place to say anything. Anyone who causes a rift between husband and wife ends up the villain – or villainess – of the piece.' Spiteful old biddy, probably consumed with jealousy, thought Falconer as the old lady finally ran out of steam.

'And you think you may not have been the only one aware of this liaison?'

'It's certainly a possibility, with one as nosy as he was.' (She could talk. Cheek!) 'But how will you find out if he was on to them?'

'I shall ask them, Miss Cadogan. I shall ask them.' With this, Falconer rose and beckoned to Carmichael to join him. There was work to be done and no time to waste.

As they showed themselves off the property, Martha Cadogan smiled to herself, well pleased with her morning's work.

'Next door, sir?' asked Carmichael, as they closed the garden gate behind them.

'That's the ticket, Sergeant. I think we'll leave the Brigadier, and tackle Lady Godiva after the village "swingers".' He knew he had used that last description incorrectly, but he was feeling frivolous and didn't give a damn.

III

Repeated knocking and ringing brought no response from The Beehive, but remembering what Miss Cadogan had said, Falconer indicated to Carmichael to follow him round to the back of the property. There, they found a wide lawn, shaded towards the rear by a vast cedar tree, beyond which the garden narrowed into an 'L' shape. Beyond this could be glimpsed a smallish whitewashed building that adjoined the rear wall. Between them and what could only be Cassandra Romaine's studio stood a cluster of some half-a-dozen beehives, from which emanated a hum that sounded almost electrical and, to the two policemen, decidedly threatening.

'What do we do now, sir,' enquired Carmichael, only to receive a stentorian 'Shhh' in reply. Falconer was rattled.

'Why are you shushing me, sir?'

'Do bees react to sound, Sergeant?'

'Don't know, sir.'

'Do you want to find out?'

'Don't think so, sir.'

'Then shut up.'

This futile exchange was saved from further protraction by the appearance of a female figure, in the doorway at the side of the little building. 'Can I help? I saw you through the end window. Not quite a true north light, but it's the best we can manage. I hope you haven't let the bees worry you. They're sweeties really.'

Cassandra Romaine was forty or so, but still retained most of the bloom and vitality of a much younger woman. Today she was swathed in vibrant pinks and purples in a boho style, and her wrists and neck clinked with chains, beads and braided threads. Her auburn hair housed more braided threads of colour, and on her tiny feet she wore dainty gold- and copper-coloured leather sandals. As she approached them through the hives they were able to appreciate how tiny she was – barely five feet in height – and, with his first close-up glimpse of her features, Falconer could appreciate why any man would find her attractive.

Her skin was tanned, her nose covered in an attractive band of freckles, her eyes a vivid green flecked with gold. When he introduced himself to her, she offered him a dainty hand with coral-painted nails. Each finger, and even the thumb, bore a silver ring, he noted. In close proximity, Carmichael appeared a mountain of humanity, she, a pixie.

When they explained the reason for their visit she grew a little wary, but still seemed fairly relaxed, as she led them back through the garden and into a low-ceilinged sitting room, complete with many an exposed beam. One wall housed a fair-sized inglenook fireplace and the décor was unexpected in its paleness. Cream carpet covered the floor, the walls and ceiling were white, the woodwork and curtains cream. The seating was in cream leather, the cushions a pinky-cream velvet.

The Romaine children obviously spent the bulk of their time at boarding school, or the upkeep of such a light colour scheme would have been an impossible task. The only colour was from the walls, which were covered in artwork. Oil paintings jostled for space with watercolours, which made way for collages and screen prints. The room was a gallery, a rainbow that spoke of a love of colour, of varied media, of vibrancy.

Falconer could not help but be impressed. Carmichael looked around in puzzlement. *Where was the television?*

The artist left them for a few moments looking round in appreciation, and returned with a laden tray. 'Earl Grey?' she asked, directing them to be seated.

After establishing that she knew Reg Morley well enough to say good-day to, and knew much of the unpleasant side of his character, the part of the interview that Falconer thought would prove uncomfortable and embarrassing proved to be no problem at all. Faced with the question of her relationship with her neighbour, Piers Manningford, she gave a little tinkling laugh and looked at Falconer with a conspiratorial air.

'Oh, you must keep this to yourself if you can, Inspector. I know Martha's generally a discreet old bird, and Piers's wife wouldn't notice for a week if he disappeared off the face of the earth, but my Clive would create like merry hell if he thought I was being a naughty girl. But, there, you won't tell him, will you? It can't have anything to do with that nasty murder, and what he doesn't know won't hurt him. After all, it's just a bit of fun, not real life.'

Falconer tried not to look scandalised at this lax attitude to morals within marriage, and asked her if she had seen Morley at all on Sunday.

'Well, not exactly seen. More heard.'

'What, you mean having a row with someone?'

'No. In the woods. He saw us. I think he was watching when we were – you know.'

Carmichael blushed as he made notes. At his age he considered Cassandra Romaine to be practic-

94

ally elderly, and what she was inferring sounded downright disgusting to one of his tender years. Falconer, his face a rigid mask to hide his disapproval, requested that she make herself a little more clear.

'With it being Sunday, you see?'

Falconer did not see, and Carmichael simply did not want to.

'Well, Clive doesn't go into the office on a Sunday, and Dorothy – Piers's wife – was at home working on some stuffy old design. What with the heat and everything – well you know what that does to one's libido. And I called Piers because I just couldn't wait until Monday, and we obviously couldn't use the studio, so I said I was going for a walk, and he said he was going to watch the hang gliders.' (Here she giggled at their subterfuge). 'And I went off down Church Street and cut off through the woods, and he went off down the Carsfold Road and cut through by the bungalows.'

'I think we get the picture, Mrs Romaine.' Falconer halted the narrative before he had to loosen his tie. 'And Mr Morley saw you, did he?'

'There's this little spot,' she continued, completely without embarrassment, 'just under this gorgeous oak tree...'

'Did Mr Morley see you, Mrs Romaine?'

'Yes. Well, I think he did. At least, someone did. We heard them. And there was a snuffling, and I just knew it was a dog. Oh, I'm sure it was him. He's always lurking in the woods on the prowl. Everyone knows what he's – what he was – like. That's why Piers originally said we had to use the studio – I've got a day bed in there, you know –

95

but it was so hot on Sunday and Clive was home, and we just couldn't wait any...'

'Thank you, Mrs Romaine,' Falconer cut her off once more. Really, the woman was a seething mass of hormones. If her husband suspected what she was up to, he probably kept quiet through sheer relief. 'Can you think of anyone who might have borne Mr Morley a grudge?'

'Just about everyone, at some time or another.' She looked thoughtful for a moment. 'Do you know about Mike Lowry?'

'Being related to him?'

'No, about when he wanted to buy the garage.' This was news. 'Go on.'

'He'd already split with Kerry by then. Her loss, I thought at the time. Good-looking man is Mike – eyes you could drown in. I would, given half a chance.' (I bet you would, thought Falconer. Carmichael almost whimpered.) 'We nearly had a thing going, you know, round about that time. He was really sweet on me, and I reckon I should have taken him up on the offer. I bet he's dynamite. I definitely missed an opportunity there.'

'Mrs Romaine.' Falconer's voice had an edge to it that could not be ignored.

'Sorry. Well, Mike wanted to buy the garage when the lease came up and he needed a loan. He knew he wouldn't make much while he built the business up, and probably wouldn't be able to afford bank rates. Anyway, even with the family rift, he thought that blood might be thicker than water, and he was pretty desperate to get his hands on the garage. So, off he went to see Great-uncle Reg, cap in hand. Got turned down flat, and had to go to the bank in the end. And what with interest payments, that's when he started to get grief from Kerry over him not paying the maintenance and, I must admit, that's when I started to lose interest. It was all beginning to look too complicated and messy, and I can do without that. I lose my inspiration if I'm distracted by trivia.'

Chapter Seven

Tuesday 14th July – morning

I

As Falconer and Carmichael headed up the drive of Pilgrims' Rest, the sound of raised voices reached them through an open window, the main protagonist being female.

'...and you did it again. You're always doing it, telling everyone what a wonderful time we have working on the house together. I heard you on the phone to that ghastly man. "Oh, real team work, pulling together, building the dream," she mimicked. '"With Dorrie's designer's eye and yours truly's manpower – hah – we're unbeatable, old son". What planet do you live on, Piers? Indoors or outdoors, whenever the slightest thing needs doing, let alone the renovation, what do you do? You whinge, you whine, you moan and complain like a ... like a petulant child. If you lift a finger it's grudgingly, and the first chance you get, you make some pathetic excuse and flounce off.'

'Dorothy, that's hardly fair...'

'Hardly fair? Do you think it's fair when I'm left on my own to work like a navvy to try to make this old wreck sound, and then to have to listen to you going on to your boring mates about how much fun it all is? Well, it's not fun, and I'm sick to death of your pathetic charade about what a good team we are. We're not. You're just a mill-stone round my neck most of the f...'

Falconer rang the bell. That sounded like the end of a round to him. If he was going to be a referee he might as well find out which colour corners they were fighting from.

The door was opened by a hard-faced woman in her late forties, her colour high, her expression creased into angry lines and furrows.

'Yes?'

About as welcoming as a spitting cobra, thought Falconer as they offered their warrant cards. Before they could speak, she spat again.

'If it's about that horrible old man getting his just desserts on Sunday, I know nothing about it. I was here. Working. If you want to know anything, ask that lazy bastard of a husband of mine. He sloped off somewhere – God knows where. I was just glad to get a bit of peace and quiet to work in.' And with that she reached behind the door, grabbed a shoulder bag, and elbowed her way past them.

The losing half of the bout emerged through a doorway to the left of the entrance. Piers Manningford was a tall man, some years younger than his wife, dark-haired and pale-skinned, with a blue shadow already showing on the lower half of his face.

'Sorry about that,' he offered, bidding them enter and conducting them through to what was obviously his study. 'Wife's a bit temperamental. Doesn't really mean it. All blow over in no time.'

Really, thought Falconer. Mrs Manningford had sounded deadly serious to him.

The preliminaries over, Manningford admitted that he had gone out on Sunday afternoon. 'Went for a stroll. Dorothy had a rush job on – she's an interior designer, you know. Thought I'd go off and see if the hang gliders were up, as it was such a lovely day. They fly off that hill down the Carsfold Road. Quite a sight. Wouldn't mind having a go myself, someday.'

Falconer let a full minute of silence drag by, watching the pleasant, social smile on Manningford's face congeal. 'Where did you go, Mr Manningford?'

'I've just told you. I went down the Carsfold Road to watch the hang gliders.'

The inspector left a shorter silence this time, but enough for a fine dew of perspiration to appear on Manningford's upper lip and forehead.

'I'm going to ask you one more time, sir.' Falconer knew he had him on the ropes. 'And I'll give you the additional information that I already know the answer. Now, where did you go on Sunday afternoon?'

'I went for a walk.' This was going to be a slow and painful business.

'Where?' The inspector's expression strongly advised against lies or misdirection.

99

'In the woods.'

'Alone?'

(Silence.)

'Were you alone, Mr Manningford?'

'No.' Manningford's already pale skin now looked like dough.

'Who were you with?'

'A friend.'

'Mr Manningford, stop wasting my time. I'm investigating a murder here, not cross-examining for the "moral police". Who were you with?'

'Mrs Romaine from next door.'

'Rather a formal way to refer to your lover, isn't it?' Falconer's voice was becoming raised with exasperation and Piers Manningford's expression changed to one of absolute panic.

'For God's sake, keep your voice down, man. Someone might hear.'

'But someone did hear on Sunday, didn't they, sir?' Falconer was always slightly dangerous when he addressed someone thus.

'Good grief. Do you know what would happen to me if Dorothy found out? This is *her* house. It'd be the end of me.'

'Then you'd better tell us about it, sir, and trust to our discretion.'

'What do you mean, discretion?'

'If it has no connection with the current investigation then the information will be kept confidential.'

Manningford's relief was almost palpable and Falconer continued while he had the advantage. 'Mrs Romaine said that your assignation was overheard, possibly even witnessed, by the deceased.

Do you confirm this?'

'There was someone.'

'Just someone?'

'It could have been anyone. It could even have been our imagination – the work of guilty consciences.' Falconer seriously doubted that Cassandra Romaine would recognise a pang of conscience if it jumped up and bit her.

'But you couldn't positively identify that someone as Mr Morley?'

'No.'

'And where were you on Sunday evening?'

'I was here.'

'All evening?'

'Yes.'

'Can anyone confirm that?'

'Yes. My wife was here working in her study. She uses one of the spare bedrooms.'

As they headed back to the car Carmichael commented, 'I thought he was going to shit a brick when he realised he'd been rumbled.'

'He'll shit more than that,' retorted Falconer, 'when he realises that he's just given himself a first-class motive for murder. No, I can't see our Mr Manningford getting out of this one unscathed, whatever the truth of the matter.'

II

The clock on the church tower was tolling one when Falconer manoeuvred his ego-mobile into a minute parking space in the main village.

'Shall we take a break for a bite, sir? Me

101

stomach thinks me throat's cut.'

The inspector stared balefully at his dark-clad companion and, while agreeing with the suggestion, thought that Carmichael's garb made him appear more suited to supping a litre or two of blood than to any more solid fare.

'Good thinking. You nip into the teashop and see what they've got. I'll go to the general store for some chilled cans and we'll sit on the Green, where we can talk with a modicum of privacy.'

'Bacon roll or three for me, then. What about you, sir?'

'Heaven forbid. A salad bap, I think. Dry – no butter. Got to look after the arteries.'

Why? thought Carmichael, unfurling himself like a giant bat from the confines of the car seat. *What harm could a little crispy bacon do?*

Falconer sauntered off to Allsorts thinking nostalgically of the ginger beer of his youth and, literally, ran into Martha Cadogan at the counter. The collision caused the old lady's bag to fall, spilling tins and packets on to the floor.

'Miss Cadogan, please accept my apologies,' he said hurriedly, bending to retrieve items rolling in opposite directions. 'I was miles away – I say, what have we here? Kittichunks? Either this is a new flavour of dog food or you've got a cat I don't know about. What's this one? "Spike's Dinner." Is this for Buster? *And* wild bird food? Are you thinking of opening a pet shop?'

Her white curls tilted to one side, Miss Cadogan's face creased in a delighted smile as she hastened to educate him. 'The cat food is for the feral cats. You always get those in agricultural areas. Sometimes – especially if the mum's just had kits – they have a hard time of it. I always put out a bowl for them night and morning to do what I can to help out. And Spike's Dinner is hedgehog food. You shouldn't give them bread and milk, it's not good for them, although a lot of folk do. And I like to watch the birds, so I keep their table well stocked. Buster's food is already safely at home in the cupboard.'

Picking up the last can, Falconer found himself posing a question. 'Don't the cats eat the hedge-hog food and vice-versa?'

'Does it matter, young man, so long as the hungry ones are fed?'

'No, I suppose not. But this must cost you a fortune.' This was an observation he would have been better keeping to himself, for she bridled and her cheeks flushed.

'Inspector Falconer, not only do I have my state pension, for which I paid all my working life, I also have my teaching pension. There are precious few pleasures left in life when one gets to be my age – which you'll discover in time to come – and what I choose to spend my money on is between me and my conscience, and no busi-ness whatsoever of anyone else.'

'I'm so sorry. I didn't mean to cause offence.' It was Falconer's turn to be embarrassed. 'You're country born and bred, and I'm a townie. I'm just not used to such generosity of spirit to wildlife in general. Please forgive me, Miss Cadogan. I had no right to say what I did.'

His blustering softened the old lady and she smiled again. 'No harm done, I'm sure. Animals are so uncomplicated, and so often get a raw deal from life – rather like young children – maybe that's why I like to feel that I do my bit to help them on their way.'

'If we were all like you, Miss Cadogan,' (Falconer recognised a truce when he was offered one) 'the world would be a better place.'

'Bless you, young man.' He held the door open for her, before returning to the counter to see about something with which to quench his embarrassment as well as his thirst.

III

He found Carmichael sitting on a bench next to the war memorial on the Green, a greasy napkin encasing a half-eaten bacon roll in his hands, and ketchup round his mouth. On the seat next to him sat a pristine napkin holding what was presumably Falconer's dry salad bap.

'You should've 'ad the bacon, sir,' his sergeant opined. 'It's that crispy it fair explodes on your taste buds.' He continued to chew noisily as the inspector gave a slight shudder, and handed him a cold draught with which to wash it down.

So much for privacy for discussion. When they rose to dispose of their litter some ten minutes later, hardly a word had been spoken. 'Mouth, Carmichael.'

'Mouth, sir?'

'Wipe it.'

'Sir?'

'Ketchup, sergeant. Wipe your mouth before

104

you get rid of the napkin. You look like a blasted vampire.'

'Sorry, sir.'

'So am I, Carmichael. So am I.'

IV

Falconer directed that the afternoon be spent visiting Mrs Rollason at the teashop (probably a good time as lunchtime was nearly over and trade should be slackening), and then strolling up to The Old Manor House for a word with Brigadier Malpas-Graves about his near-fisticuffs in The Fisherman's Flies, and his visit to Crabapple Cottage on Sunday evening. That should give them an interesting time. Then, perhaps, they could head back to the office, pick over the bones of all they'd learnt, and plan out how they were going to play 'round two'.

Once inside the cool interior of the teashop, Falconer introduced himself, adding, 'And you must be Mrs Rollason, the 999 caller.'

From behind the counter Rebecca beamed a smile at Carmichael, greeting him like an old friend. 'Back again so soon, Davey? My rolls must be better than I thought.' Turning to Falconer she continued, 'And you must be the dry salad bap.'

Such directness caught the inspector offside. He murmured, 'I suppose I must be,' and tried to put the interview on a more formal footing, missing the twinkle in the young woman's eyes at his discomfiture. His manner, therefore, was very formal as he ran through the events of the previous morning that had culminated in her 999 call. Nothing new, however, was added to what was already known, and her narrative merely confirmed Alan Warren-Browne's angry assault on the old man's door, followed by a short absence, then his return to the front of the property to blurt out his grisly discovery.

'What about the previous day? Did you hear or see anything of Mr Morley? Did he have any callers that you noticed?' Maybe there would be something new here.

'I saw him go out in the afternoon, and there were words then.'

'Go on.' Carmichael flipped open his notebook. Encased in black plastic, it matched the rest of his expanse and went unnoticed. Even his pen was black.

'We'd had a lovely, lazy few hours in the garden – we live next door at The Rookery. We don't stay open for Sunday lunches – we leave that to the pub to cater for – and Nick, that's my husband, got on with mowing the lawns while Tristram and I came in here to open up.'

'Tristram?' queried Falconer, simultaneously looking down in reaction to a light pressure on his right lower leg. His gaze met that of a very small person, a very small, sticky person, using his trouser leg as a ladder to achieve an upright stance. The very small, sticky person flashed a dazzling smile upwards, before being swept off his feet and into his mother's arms.

'Oh, you little beast! Have you got yourself covered in jam again? You're a little tinker, so you are,' cooed Rebecca, who held her son aloft and explained to his erstwhile ladder, 'This is Tristram. Isn't he a darling?'

Falconer gave an insincere smile of agreement as he surveyed the ruin of his lower trouser leg, and urged her to continue.

'We'd just opened up and I'd waved to Martha – that's Miss Cadogan – who was having a sit in the sun on the Green, and I was laying the tables in the front window. I heard Buster yapping, and then Kerry from next door to Mr Morley opened a window and shouted something at him as he was going out.' This was confirmation of what Kerry Long had told him herself, the previous day.

'Did you catch what was said?'

'Not word for word, like, but it was something to do with Buster and his toilet habits. Not the first time his habits have caused trouble, but probably the last, as I understand that Buster's now up at The Old School House. Martha'll keep him on the straight and narrow. He'll be well looked after there.'

'That's all?'

'I think Buster must have got into Kerry's garden again and left a little present. She reckoned that old Morley put him in there when she was at work just to rile her, but we'll never know now. That was it, just a warning shot across his bows, from what I can remember. I was more concerned with keeping this busy little bee out of my honeypots, wasn't I, pudding?' With this, she poked her son in the ribs and he responded with a cascade of delighted laughter at this unexpected attention.

'What about later in the day?'

'No.' The young woman looked thoughtful, and

then her eyes widened. 'Yes, he did have a visitor.' Her memory jolted, she continued. 'Nick had gone to the pub for a couple of pints to end the weekend, and I was in the kitchen getting a bottle for this little tinker who'd just woken up.'

'What time was this?'

Again, a pause. 'It was nine o'clock. I remember because the church clock had just struck the hour when I went into the kitchen. I happened to glance out of the window – it wasn't fully dark – and I saw someone outside his front door.'

'Have you any idea who it might have been?'

'Let me look at it again,' and she closed her eyes, then said, 'Yes. It was the Brigadier. It must have been him because of the stick.'

'The stick?'

'Yes. The Brigadier always carries a walking stick – silver-topped one it is, used to belong to his father. He had a stick, so it must've been him.'

Marvelling at what he perceived to be female logic, Falconer nevertheless added this little snippet to his 'to do' list and pressed on. 'We have been told that Mr Morley was a bit of a voyeur. Do you know anything in this regard?'

'A bit of a what?'

'A voyeur. Liked to spy on people. A bit of a peeping tom,' he explained.

At this the young woman blushed and turned away, her good humour momentarily quenched. 'S'pose he was.' She was defensive now. 'Used to spy on us when we were courting. He did it to all the local couples, not just us, but that was just his way.' She ground to a halt.

Falconer let the silence draw out for nearly a

108

minute to increase the tension, before he cut to the chase.

'Nothing more recent that you recall?'

No reply. Rebecca made a play of straightening Tristram's romper suit and pushing back his fringe.

'Nothing regarding yourself?' Even Carmichael was squirming now.

With an attempt at belligerence that did not quite come off, she turned towards him and blurted out, 'So what if he did spy on me a bit? He's dead now, so it's hardly going to happen again, is it? So the matter's closed.'

'Did you or your husband speak to Mr Morley about his intrusive behaviour?' Falconer could match her, snit for snit.

'When Nick told me that Martha Cadogan had more or less caught him red-handed in the back lane, I told him to leave it be. I should have made sure the curtains were closed. I didn't want any trouble, and Nick said he'd leave it. That was it.'

Was it now? thought Falconer, remembering what Kerry Long had told him. 'You said your husband went to the local pub for a drink on Sunday night? What time did he get in?'

Not seeing any connection between this and the previous questions, Rebecca looked relieved and answered without hesitation. 'About a quarter past ten.'

109

Chapter Eight

Tuesday 14th July – early afternoon

I

The Old Manor House really was old, the original building having been constructed during the reign of the first Elizabeth. Although added to over the centuries, the additions had been sympathetic to the original style and it faced the world, a gracious confection of beams, mullioned windows, leaded lights and fancy brickwork. Several barley-sugar-twist chimneys sprouted from its gabled roof, and its slight air of shabbiness merely enhanced its charm.

Its main door was unexpectedly large: heavy oak blackened with age and wear, and heavily studded. To its right hung an old-fashioned bell-pull, which Falconer viewed with some suspicion. Such objects had been known to come off in his hand before now. He decided to take no chances and indicated to Carmichael to give it a tug. The resultant dull clang was in perfect sympathy with the younger man's funereal appearance, and the scene would have made a suitable opening for a horror film.

The door opened to reveal a well-preserved man with a venerable paunch, who could have been any age from sixty-five to eighty. Brigadier Godfrey

Malpas-Graves was, in fact, seventy-seven years of age, but was extraordinarily active for a man of his vintage. Of above-average height, he had neatly cut, short greyish-white hair and an expertly clipped white beard. His clothing, although casual, was immaculate and, as he offered a greeting to the callers, his still-blue eyes twinkled a welcome.

'Police chappies? Thought so. Godfrey Malpas-Graves at your service. Come on through. Don't mind if I carry on with the gardening while we talk, do you? Wife and I are doing a spot of tidying in the old veg patch. Daren't leave it a day or old Mother Nature'll be in there wreaking havoc with her blasted weeds.'

As they completed the introductions, he preceded them through the house, and back out by a side door that led to an extensive kitchen garden. Row upon row of plants were interwoven with narrow pathways, beans scaled dizzying heights on a complicated arrangement of canes, and at one end sprouted a profusion of netted soft fruit bushes and strawberry beds. A further enclosure of wire housed a number of hens and a belligerent and very vocal cockerel.

At their approach, a woman rose from her kneeling position next to a trug half-full of already wilting weeds. Although dressed in a light summer frock and sandals, she wore stout gardening gloves and held a trowel in her right hand.

'Joyce. Police chappies here to see us about that old reprobate, Morley.'

'Really, Godfrey, that's hardly appropriate language, given the circumstances.'

111

'Speak as I find, my dear, speak as I find. Should know that after all these years. By the way, this is Inspector Falconer, and this sinister chappie here is Acting DS Carmichael. You wearing that outfit for a bet, sonny?'

Falconer cleared his throat loudly and asked them if they knew anything that could throw light on Reg Morley's demise.

'Not a thing, old boy, I'm afraid.'

'But we have heard that the old chap was loaded,' Joyce cut in, a steely glint in her eyes. 'Buckets of money found in the cottage, and him as mean as old Scrooge himself.'

'And helping himself from our garden, whenever the whim took him.'

'Excuse me,' Falconer interrupted. 'How did you know about money being found?'

'Everyone knows. Village grapevine. Fastest growing plant around. Wish these blighters were as fast-growing, I can tell you,' he explained, tilting his head towards his own produce.

'Buckets and buckets of money,' continued his wife, not wanting to let the matter drop. 'How much was it exactly, Inspector?'

Falconer decided to wait until he had more time to give Proudfoot as good a verbal working-over as he was ever likely to get, and gave by way of scant explanation, 'Let's just say it was a considerable amount, Mrs Malpas-Graves.'

'Party pooper!'

'I beg your pardon?' Had he really heard that?

'Nothing, Inspector. Just clearing my throat.'

'To continue, I understand that you had a bit of a run-in with Mr Morley in The Fisherman's

Flies last Friday, Brigadier. Would you be so good as to tell me about it?'

The older man harrumphed a bit and coloured slightly, before beginning his narrative. 'Feel rather ashamed about it in retrospect. Damned silly thing to do, but I'd had a few little snifters, and that old sod had been at my fruit and veg yet again. When he started to make snide comments, I just lost my rag.'

'He's like that, you know,' his wife commented almost absently. Her gimlet eye had just fallen on a clump of chickweed over by the lettuces, and she was eager to eradicate it. 'Loses it easily, but it never lasts long. Quick to anger, quick to cool, is Godfrey,' she concluded, sidling away from them to uproot her quarry.

'We must've looked a right pair of old fools,' her husband continued with his narrative, 'squaring up to each other like that. It's just as well George Covington had the good sense to step in when he did. All in all, made a bit of an ass of myself.'

'And that was it, was it? You didn't try to tackle him about it again, did you?'

Carmichael had sat himself down on a sawn-off tree stump and was busily scribbling in his note-book, a petulant scowl on his face at the Brigadier's earlier description of him.

'Don't think so, old chap, don't think so.'

'Well do you think you could think again, and tell me what you were doing at the door of Crab-apple Cottage at nine o'clock on Sunday evening?'

The Brigadier's eyes popped wide open as he observed, 'I say, you have been doing your home-work, haven't you? Caught me out fair and square

113

with that one.'

'Go on.'

'I was there, and it was at nine o'clock. Heard the clock strike as I was trying to make myself heard at the door. Thought I ought to have it out with him properly. He'd had my asparagus and my soft fruits – hardly the choice of a hungry man, more that of a greedy man.'

'And what did Mr Morley have to say about this?'

'Oh, I never spoke to him. I hammered on the door a few times, but I could hear raised voices coming from round the back, and presumed someone else was getting their twopenn'orth in. So I came home.'

'And the next we heard he was dead,' Joyce concluded for him.

'Did you see anyone else about, when you were there?'

'Only... No, no, sorry, no one. Never saw a soul.'

'Are you absolutely certain about that?' (Would you like to phone a friend?)

'Got there at nine. No one about. Bashed the door a bit, then walked back home. Not a soul around.'

'Thank you, Brigadier. No doubt we'll speak again.'

As they left The Old Manor House Falconer turned to Carmichael and said, 'We've not got the full story from that old cove. We'll leave him to stew for a bit, and then I'll see if I can get him to trip himself up. But for now, I'd like another word with that Lowry chap, ask him about trying to tap his great-uncle for a loan. Money's always an excellent bet for motive in any murder case.'

'So's sex, sir,' added his sergeant, eager to display his knowledge.

'Yes, Carmichael, but hardly in this case.'

Chapter Nine

Tuesday 14th July – afternoon

I

School was already out for the day, and the near-emptiness of the village earlier had changed with the arrival of the school bus. As Falconer and Carmichael skirted the village green, a group of teenagers lounged on the benches smoking, the boys showing off, hoping to impress the girls by chasing the ducks, or by displaying the pretend intent to 'duck' one of the fairer sex in the green waters of the pond. A trio of younger children sat in the welcome shade of one of the massive oaks, giving their complete concentration to the task of manufacturing daisy chains, oblivious to the horseplay of those a few years their senior. Outside the teashop, a couple of young mothers with pushchairs had stopped to chat with each other and, in the distance, a dog barked intermittently.

Turning off into Drovers Lane, these signs of life ceased, however, and no through traffic spoilt its calm. It was, then, completely out of keeping with the tranquillity of the scene, that three sharp cracks rang out from the direction of the rear of the garage, and the two men unconsciously increased their pace in pursuit of the source of these reports.

Rounding the garage shop and pumps and entering the rear workshop bay, they found the proprietor taking his ease on a pile of worn tyres near the rear perimeter wall, a cigarette (surely dangerous) in one hand, an air pistol in the other. Seeing them approach, he greeted them with barely concealed contempt. 'Well, if it isn't Sherlock bleedin' Holmes again. And who is your lovely companion for today? Herman Munster, as I live and breathe. What have you come to waste my time with today?'

'We'd like another word with you about your relations with your great-uncle, sir.' Falconer was coldly formal, as he dusted off his dander, prior to erecting it. Carmichael, trying his best for a contemptuous sneer and failing, merely glowered and silently produced his notebook. 'But before we do that, exactly what are you doing with that air pistol? Isn't it a little dangerous discharging it a, near flammable substances, and b, in an area into which anyone could wander at any time, and into which we just did?'

'Missed you, didn't I? And for your information Mr Policeman, a, I know where not to fire it, and b, I know *when* not to fire it. And to answer your first question last, I've got to keep the rats down somehow, and they don't all go for the poison I lay down. So I get a bit of target practice – so what? They're only vermin. I can assure you I don't shoot pigs, no matter what the provocation,' this last ignored, but recognised as intentionally inflammatory.

'You lay poison out here?' Carmichael looked disturbed. 'What about cats and the like? Isn't it dangerous for them?'

'Occasionally. Tough, though, innit? Usually just the odd feral cat, and they don't have much of a life anyway, so I reckon I'm doing them a service. Forget it and let's get on with what you've come about. I don't want you wasting any more of my time than you have to. Some of us have got a living to earn.'

Carmichael looked down at his waiting note-book, an expression of contempt and disgust on his face. He knew rats needed keeping down, but Lowry did not seem to mind what took the bait. Falconer, with a blank expression, took up the reins. 'Do you own this garage, Mr Lowry?'

'I own a short-term lease on it.'

'And how did you finance the purchase of that lease?'

'Is that any of your damned business?'

'At present, I rather think it is.'

'What possible bearing could that have on the old boy's death? I think you're just being bloody nosy.'

'You can think what you like. I think the answer may be important to this investigation, and if you're not prepared to answer my questions freely here, then maybe you had better accompany us to Market Darley and we can continue this conversation there on a more formal footing.'

'OK, point taken,' Lowry capitulated with a bad grace. 'I got a bank loan. Didn't have much

117

in the way of savings, so I've hocked myself to the moneylenders.'

'To the official moneylenders, Mr Lowry. But first of all, didn't you try to obtain money from an unofficial moneylender?'

'I don't know what you're talking about.' The air of challenge had left him. He no longer looked Falconer in the eye, and was beginning to bluster. 'I borrowed it from the bank fair and square. Where else is someone like me going to lay their hands on a lump sum like that?'

'Perhaps from his great-uncle, sir.'

'What do you mean? What are you implying?'

'Do you deny that you approached Mr Morley in the hope of securing a personal loan, to avoid the steep interest charges incurred by a loan from a bank?'

'I don't...'

'And do you deny that he turned you down flat, and that was the reason you were forced to accept finance from the bank?'

'Who told you this? Where did you get this from? Oh, I know, it was that Romaine tart, wasn't it? She's the only one would say anything about that. Cheap little tramp. Did she turn a trick for you, Inspector, or wouldn't even she stoop to that? Poking and prying into other people's private business – how can you stoop so low?'

'How could anyone stoop so low as to murder an elderly man in his own kitchen?' countered Falconer. 'Now, for the last time, did you approach your great-uncle for a loan, Mr Lowry? I shan't ask you again.'

'I was his only living relative,' he said, casually

118

ignoring the existence of his own two children, 'I knew he had it, mean old skinflint, and he sent me away with a flea in my ear. Laughed, he did, when I pleaded with him. His only living relative and he turned me away. Well, much good it'll do him now. There are no pockets in a shroud.'

'Indeed there are not, Mr Lowry. And your great-uncle would need very large pockets indeed to hold what we found upstairs under his bed. Nine thousand pounds, Mr Lowry, is what we found. And you say you're his only living relative? I suppose you've just conveniently forgotten the existence of your sons?'

II

As they turned to take their leave, they were almost bowled over by a furious-looking Kerry Long, dragging in her wake two children aged about five and six. 'Daddy, Daddy,' they chorused, pulling free and hurtling towards him to grab him round the waist and be shooed away back towards their mother.

'Don't you "Daddy" him, the tight-fisted, good-for-nothing,' she grated, preparing to launch into a full, bitter flood.

'Slowly, Carmichael,' hissed Falconer, dropping his progress to a snail's pace. 'Walk very slowly, and when we get to the corner we're going to slip round there and see what we can hear.' And with this somewhat confusing instruction, he tugged on his sergeant's T-shirt to guide him out of sight, but still within earshot. It was like

119

trying to tow a small mountain.

'Where were you yesterday, then? You were supposed to bring round the maintenance but, as usual, you were nowhere to be seen. You know damned well that both these two need new shoes, and I haven't even got their school dinner money this week. And how do you think it's going to look come Thursday, when I won't even have the cash for them to go swimming with their class-mates?'

'Hold up there, Kerry, I can't give you what I haven't got, can I? And I was a bit distracted yes-terday, what with old Uncle Reg getting the chop...'

'Oh, so it's old Uncle Reg now, is it? How con-venient. It was "that miserable old bastard" before. You can change your tune when the mood takes you, can't you?'

'Be fair, Kerry.'

'Be fair? Be fair? When were you ever fair to me or to these two kids of yours? I do what I can, but I don't get paid till Friday, and I'll not ask Auntie for another sub. It's all she can do to keep her head above water, without me sponging off her.'

'Well, what do you expect me to do?'

'Give me my bloody maintenance, that's what I expect you to do. This time is the last straw. Uncle Alan says he's going to speak to his solicitor so that you're legally bound, and Auntie said you'd better get used to shopping in Carsfold for your gro-ceries. She might be struggling, but she said she'd rather go under than serve the likes of you again.'

'Where am I supposed to get the money from, then, girl?'

'Let's try the till for a start. There should be a few pounds in that by this time of day.'

'Come on, Carmichael,' said Falconer in muted tones. 'Show's over. Let's make ourselves scarce before we're caught out as the pair of dirty eavesdroppers that we are.'

Chapter Ten

Tuesday 14th July – afternoon

I

Back in their office in Market Darley, Falconer and Carmichael, with the twin aids of memory and the sergeant's notebook, went through what they had got so far 'to see if there were any favourites running' as Falconer had put it. The inspector leaned back in his chair, feet on desk, as the sergeant hunched over his notes in concentration.

'Right then, who's an obvious non-starter, Carmichael? What do you say?'

'Well, those two at the pub don't seem to've had any grudge against the old chap. That bit of business in the bar with the Brigadier's nothing to an experienced publican, which he obviously is.'

'Well done. Who else is out of the running?'

'Can't see the old lady being in the frame either, can you sir?'

'Old Mother Cadogan? No. She might not have been over-fond of the old boy, but he seems to have steered well clear of her. Perhaps he knew when he'd met his match. What do you say to the Swainton-Smythes – the Rev. Smug and his gossiping gush of a wife?' asked Falconer, rising to open another window and encourage a through draught.

'He seems too other-worldly. Not the type. Doesn't seem to want to hear a bad word about anybody.'

'He got to the body before us, though didn't he? He could've been in there destroying evidence for someone else, even if he didn't do it himself – secrets of the confessional and all that.'

'That's Catholics, sir. And do you really think he'd've done that?'

'Nah. Go on. You're doing fine.'

'I can't say I can see any motive for his wife either, can you?'

Falconer eased his feet back on to his desk. 'That old man caused quite a bit of ill-feeling in the church,' he offered. 'Rev. DD lets it all wash over him, but she's a completely different kettle of fish. There's a lot of emotion simmering just below the surface with that one, and she's fiercely protective of her husband: treats him almost like her child in some ways. What say she did away with the old man to make her husband's life less stressful? Stranger things have happened.' Without giving Carmichael the chance to answer, he went on, 'What do you think about the postmaster? He who finds the body has to be just a little bit suspect.'

Carmichael looked thoughtful. 'He does pander to that wife of his, doesn't he, sir? And they're both very concerned with their god-daughter's welfare. And the old man goaded him whenever he had the chance. I suppose he could have been pushed over the edge. It does happen in neighbour disputes.'

'Well done, Sergeant.' Falconer was experiencing what felt like the beginnings of a partnership here. 'Now let's move on to said god-daughter. She had a whole heap of reasons to dislike her neighbour. He led her a terrible dance, one way and another – his behaviour, from what we've heard, was enough to goad anyone beyond endurance, let alone a working single parent struggling to raise two children.'

'She's doing a very good job, sir.' (Warning, warning! Extreme danger!)

But Falconer waded in where angels feared to tread. 'Don't let sentimentality cloud your judgement, Carmichael,' he warned. 'She had that old git next door, the kids, a job to hold down, no washing machine, and next to no support, financial or otherwise, from that ex- of hers. And if the ex- had secured a loan from Morley, he wouldn't have had to meet high repayment rates and, maybe, her life would have been a little easier – Lowry not working all hours to make ends meet, maintenance payments a bit more regular. Maybe that last incident with the dog excrement was the straw that broke the camel's back.'

'You're barking up the wrong tree there. She's a nice young woman and Lowry was a fool to let her go.'

'Oh, wake up and smell the coffee, Carmichael. Take off those rose-coloured spectacles before you break into song. This is real life, not *The*

Sound of Music.'

After a silent stand-off that lasted for some minutes, Falconer resumed the précis. 'What about Mrs Romaine, and/or Manningford?'

'I don't rate her, sir.' Carmichael had calmed down a bit, and was willing to come out to play again.

'Boy, was she a bitch on heat.' Falconer wrinkled his nose in distaste at the memory.

'But she didn't care, did she? She didn't seem all that bothered about her bit of hanky-panky coming out.'

'Indeed she did not, but lover boy wasn't quite so sanguine, was he? He was definitely terrified about his wife finding out what he had been up to. And if she's got all the money, he's got an awful lot to lose.'

'And the old man was spying on them in the woods. Maybe he'd already put the squeeze on.'

'And he went over to see Morley,' continued Falconer, taking over the theory, 'maybe just to beg for his discretion, the old man laughed in his face, and bingo.'

'Nice one, sir.'

'Thank you, sergeant. Now, who does that leave?'

'What about the Brigadier?'

'Yes. Got a quick temper, that one. He'd already had a run in with the old man in the pub, and he was still losing his produce. Plus, he didn't volunteer that he'd been down to the old man's cottage that evening. I've got a feeling the old devil's still hiding something, and I'm going to find out exactly what it is and face him with it.

'Now, who's left? The Wilson woman who runs the shop? She's Ms Long's aunt, so has a strong interest in her welfare. She was owed a large-ish amount of money by Morley, and is struggling to keep that business of hers afloat. It may have been enough for her to snap.' Goodness, what incestuous breeding grounds of resentment and hostility villages are, he thought: all tranquil on the surface, but absolutely seething with emotion underneath.

'And we haven't spoken to that Rollason chap either, sir,' Carmichael reminded him. 'Do you remember Kerry – Ms Long – said she'd seen him walking away from the old man's door,' (here he consulted his notebook on two separate pages) 'a little after nine, but his wife said he didn't get in until ten fifteen.'

'Good point, good point. We'll start with him when we get there tomorrow. And that just leaves us with great-nephew Michael Lowry, crack shot and neglectful father. He looks like an odds-on favourite to me.'

'He wouldn't have tried to borrow from the old man if he didn't think he had a tidy sum tucked away.'

'Nor would he, Carmichael. Life would be running a lot more smoothly for him if Morley had given him some financial backing. And whatever grief the old man inflicted on his ex-wife and children would just be served up cold as extra aggravation for him. We've got quite a full race card here. Let's hope some of them start falling at the fences soon, so that we can see the wood for the trees, as it were.' Good grief! he thought, this conversation was heading for Cliché City if

125

he didn't take more care.

'Right, that's enough of that. I suggest we put in an hour or so going through that glorious collection of litter we brought back with us.'

Most of the papers were easy to discard, consisting mainly of old household bills and receipts. In the detritus were also the few official documents that covered the span of the old man's lifetime: his birth certificate, birth and death certificates for his wife, their marriage certificate, paid-off mortgage papers and the deeds to the property.

Falconer also found a pile of personal letters, yellowed with age and beginning to come apart where they had lain folded for so long, but he expected to learn little of recent events from these, and set them aside for perusal on the morrow.

Circulars advertising special offers, and an enormous assortment of junk mail were also discarded, as they should have been the minute they came through the letterbox. What was it about the ageing process, he wondered, that turned people into squirrels? Why should they suddenly find it necessary to hoard every scrap of what they had, in earlier life, thrown away instantly?

A 'sir' from Carmichael made him look up. 'I think you'd better come and have a look at this. I don't know if it's legal, but it looks like a will to me.'

Falconer was on his feet in an instant and hurried over to the sergeant's desk, taking the tattered sheet of paper from him. 'If I've got any relatives left,' Falconer squinted to make out the crabbed copperplate handwriting, faded ink on age-discoloured paper, 'then they can have what I've got. I might hate my family but I fair despises the government and they ain't getting what I've scraped together in my lifetime.' It was signed, in the same shaky hand, Reginald Ernest Morley, and bore two more signatures as witness – those of a John and Catherine Marchant – and dated some ten years earlier.

'Well, well, well, there's a turn-up for the books. We'll have to get this checked out, but it looks kosher to me. We'll have to ask around and find out who these Marchants were. I'll try the Reverend Snotty first and, if he doesn't know, I'll ask at the pub. Someone ought to remember them. And we know who Morley's only living adult relative is, don't we, Carmichael? And we know he has no alibi for Sunday night and that he's strapped for cash. This just strengthens the case against him.'

'But if he killed him, why didn't he just take the money and run?' asked the sergeant.

'Use your head, man. Most of that money was in old fivers. If Lowry'd tried to change that amount of them in a bank it would've raised a few eyebrows, and it wouldn't have been long before we got to hear about it. Anyway, if he knew about the horde, maybe others did as well. No, this way was the safest. Do for him late in the evening, so that there's no chance of anyone knowing what had happened and nipping in and helping themselves, then leave the place in the safe hands of the police next morning. You can be sure that, if Alan Warren-Browne hadn't gone round when he did, Lowry would've found some excuse to call round there and "find" the body.'

'You think he knew about the will?'

'It all fits. But don't forget, what's sauce for the goose is sauce for the gander, no matter how hard you find that to swallow.' There he went again!

They fell silent once more, and continued with their search through the mouldering papers. Hardly a breeze stirred through the office, and ominous black clouds were building up in the west, heralding a stormy evening. But weather conditions went unnoticed as they scanned and discarded their way through the dwindling piles.

Falconer gave a low whistle at almost the same moment as Carmichael called for his attention once more. 'What have you got, Sergeant?'

'Bank book, sir. Very old but not cancelled.'

'How much?' Falconer held his breath.

'Four thousand, three hundred and fifteen pounds and thirty-six pence, sir. Last entry made not long after decimalization. So why haven't we found any statements then?'

'The old sinner probably burnt them in case anyone saw, and tried to tap him for a loan, as did his great-nephew, if you remember. I'll ring the bank in the morning to see what the up-to-date balance is. That four grand is probably worth two or three times as much by now.'

'What've you got?'

'One moment and I'll tell you,' and the inspector made a brief but productive phone call. As he replaced the receiver his eyes were gleaming. 'Insurance policy, Carmichael. Current value with bonuses is a little over fifteen thousand pounds. That old boy was worth at least thirty grand, and that's without taking into account the value of the property, which even in this state is going to be well over a hundred and fifty k. Worth doing murder for, don't you think? This just looks blacker and blacker for Mr Michael Lowry.'

At that point they were interrupted by the arrival of duty sergeant Bob Bryant. 'This was just dropped off for you, Inspector Falconer. Full report of the PM. Nice little facer in there. Hope you don't mind, but I had a peep.'

Falconer looked through the report. Cause of death: as thought. Time of death, somewhere between 9 pm and midnight. Wire from neck identified as that commonly available from any hardware or DIY store. Contents of stomach, partly-digested bread and cheese, something chocolaty (cocoa), and approximately three times the normal dosage of a commonly prescribed, but medically old-fashioned, sleeping tablet.

'Get on to the doctor at Castle Farthing surgery and see if – no leave it, I'll do it myself. If any of our runners was prescribed those tablets, I want to know who, when, and why. And where are the leftovers, if any?'

Chapter Eleven

Wednesday 15th July – morning

I

Falconer was in the office early the following morning, and seven-thirty found him at his desk, working his way through the personal letters that were all that was left of the Morley paperwork.

The oldest and most fragile consisted of letters that had passed between the old man and his then sweetheart, later his wife, during the Second World War, and Falconer paid these only scant attention. He felt they could have no bearing on the old man's end so many years later, and had no wish to be a voyeur on their courtship. A few letters from the immediate post-war era were from old comrades-in-arms, passing on their de-mob news, and a few – intermittently spaced – were from family members. These last he paid more attention to, as they would provide some background for the feud that had so distanced Morley from those family members and, ultimately, from his great-nephew.

It proved to be a very sorry tale indeed, a dispute arising between brothers after the death of their father. Most of the correspondence was from Reg's younger brother Robert, and centred on the name which had been shared by both Reginald Ernest Morley, died two days ago, and his late father, who had passed on in 1957. There had been several withdrawals made from Reginald Morley senior's account, in that name and with a rather dubious signature, made after the date of his demise. A sad but predictable tale, given what Falconer had learnt about the recently-deceased Reginald Ernest Morley junior: it had all been about money and greed. The rift appeared to have been final, the bank informed to freeze the account (although no documentary evidence was here available to back this up), as the letters, abusive and accusatory, tailed off after a few months, finally wishing ill for the rest of his days to the recipient.

He was about to pack away the pile when a lone piece of paper, envelope-less and folded very small and haphazardly, caught his eye. He picked it up, carefully opened it out, read, and whistled quietly to himself. 'I can't pay any more and I can't take any more. You must live with the consequences now.' That was all. The letter was unsigned and undated, but undoubtedly fairly old. Given a small leap of the imagination, however, it did suggest that some of the surprisingly large amount of money in the Morley coffers may have come by the exercise of a little local blackmail.

Most of the cash from the cache in the cottage had been in old five-pound notes, and no deposit had been made in the bank account (he must phone to verify details) for well over thirty years. Something may have happened to force the old man into early retirement – the letter was darkly suggestive of this – or maybe he had just lost his taste for the game. A quick check of Mrs Morley's

131

death certificate showed a date in 1972. That had possibly been the trigger. And then he must have lost heart, just done a bit of spying here and there. Maybe he had been stashing money away for both of them in their old age and, without his wife, it had not seemed worth the bother any more.

Whatever the story was, maybe catching Cassandra Romaine and Piers Manningford in a compromising situation in the woods, and knowing who held the purse-strings in the Manningford household, had awakened the old greed. Maybe he had just been bored. In any case, Piers Manningford had better anoint himself with oil for, after he had rattled Nick Rollason's cage, Falconer was going to give him a severe grilling.

Looking at his fob watch he noted that it was eight-thirty, and about time he left to pick up Carmichael. His eyes rolled towards the ceiling as he wondered what sight would greet him today.

II

At a toot from the horn, Carmichael ducked through the front door and made his way down the front garden, which seemed, overnight, to have added a semi-derelict caravan and wrecked Mini, partly cannibalised for parts, to its junkyard ornamentation.

Today's outfit was less funereal than the day before's, and consisted of brown. That one word summed it up. Carmichael had plumped, once more, for a single-colour ensemble. With his great height and breadth, and his slightly bovine

132

expression, Falconer could not decide whether to open the door for him or offer to fetch a milking stool.

It was scorchingly hot today, but if only the weather would break, maybe he would be able to *steer* his partner into slacks and a nice, white, long-sleeved shirt with a tie.

III

Parking at the lower end of the village they called first at the surgery to enquire about the diazepam found in Reg Morley's stomach.

They were in luck, as the surgery was only open three days a week, on Mondays, Wednesdays and Fridays. On Tuesdays, Thursdays and Saturday mornings, anyone from the village who needed to see a doctor had to make the four-mile journey to Stoney Cross, as it was a split practice. All this was explained to them by the brisk receptionist, who also informed them that today's duty doctor was Dr Philip Christmas, and that he currently had a fifteen-minute break between consultations (at this, an elderly woman seated in the waiting area glared darkly towards the receptionist and tapped her walking stick in impatience) and would see them now.

They found Dr Christmas seated before a computer monitor, a cup of black coffee in one hand, a half-eaten jam doughnut in the other.

'Come in, gentlemen, and take a seat while I wash my hands. They're covered in sugar and not fit to be shaken.'

133

He was a man in his mid-fifties, of medium height and build, with salt-and-pepper hair and a thick and luxuriant moustache, from which he surreptitiously dislodged stray crystals of sugar as he listened to their request for information.

'Normally I wouldn't feel happy about supplying you with the names of patients taking a particular medication.'

'You do see how important it may prove to this investigation, Dr Christmas? This may be the key to who was responsible for Mr Morley's death – I presume he was one of your patients too?'

'He was, and I do appreciate your position. Fortunately, in this case, there is no dilemma for me. You may know that diazepam is a somewhat outmoded drug in the fight against insomnia, and was always a problem, in that it can induce a high degree of dependence.'

Falconer nodded, indicating that he understood.

'The newer generation of hypnotics such as Zopiclone are more sophisticated, less likely to leave the patient with a chemical hangover the next morning and, if used with care and in moderation, don't generally cause problems with dependence.'

'And?'

'That's the answer to your question, gentlemen. This practice does not prescribe diazepam, nor has it for some years now. That's why I am able to answer your question without fear of breach of patient confidentiality. We simply don't have any patients being prescribed that particular drug.'

And that was the end of that line of enquiry.

What had seemed so promising a shortcut had turned into a cul-de-sac, leaving them with nowhere else to go with the stomach contents.

Or was there? Didn't Falconer remember seeing a milk pan in the sink? The cocoa mug had disappeared to forensics, and he would soon know if the drug had been in the mug. Had it also been in the saucepan too? And did it really matter? He did not know at this stage, but resolved to collect the pan and send it off to see what, if anything apart from a little mould by now, it had to offer.

And what about the wire? Who was likely to be able to lay their hands on that? Who was likely to have a ready supply? Maybe someone who worked in a garage? (He was rather vague in his thoughts on this.) Someone who hung pictures (or was there a special wire for that?) Someone who arranged flowers (florists' wire?) Someone who kept chickens, or anyone, in fact, who had a garden, or indulged in DIY? No, that was another blind alley, unless they were lucky enough to find the actual roll from which this piece was cut, and managed to match the cut ends. He would leave the wire as a last resort, as the search of a large number of houses, sheds, garages, outbuildings and gardens would require an amount of manpower likely to induce a coronary in his immediate superior, and earn him a dressing down over his own investigational incompetence.

IV

As they left the surgery, Falconer was roused from his negative musings by the sound of raised voices coming from the garage forecourt next door. Once more, he grabbed Carmichael, and guided him to a hidden position behind the dividing wall. One of those voices had to be Mike Lowry's, and anything they could get on him might prove useful, if only as a lever.

'What do you mean by calling me an over-priced cheat? You booked the service and I told you how much it would cost. Any work needed is extra, and you understood that.'

'Oh, I understood, all right. And look at the length of this worksheet.'

'It needed doing.'

'Most of it damned well didn't.'

'Are you a mechanic?'

'Are *you,* more to the point? All that I was aware needed doing was an oil change and the hand-brake tightening. I see that's on here, so let's just have a little check.' Here there was a short break in hostilities followed by a triumphant 'Aha!'

'There you go. One little shove on this slope and it moved. You can't tell me you adjusted that, and if you did, you're damned incompetent.'

'I may have been mistaken on that little detail.'

'That little detail?' The other voice, now recognisable as Piers Manningford's, rose to a shriek.

Here, a third voice broke in, accompanied by the yapping of a dog. 'Michael Lowry, Piers Manningford, whatever are you thinking of, making a show of yourselves like this in public?'

136

'You keep out of it, Miss Cadogan. This is no business of yours.' Lowry sounded no less angry, even with the arrival of the old lady.

'My business it may not be, but surely you can't be surprised that I'd rather you fell out rather more privately than next to the public highway.'

'Oh, bugger off, you interfering old biddy.'

'Michael!' This last followed a sharp yelp from the dog.

'And take that flea-ridden mutt with you or you might find he's been unlucky enough to pick up some poisoned rat bait.'

'Miss Cadogan, has he hurt Buster? Lowry, you're scum.' Piers had intervened.

'Come along, Buster, let's get you home where you'll be safe from brutes like him. You've bad blood in you, Michael Lowry. Think on, or you'll turn out just like your great-uncle.'

'How could you treat her like that, Lowry? She was only trying to make peace.'

'Now look, Manningford, why don't you visit www-dot-shut-the-fuck-up-dot-com and then just pay this bill. Apart from the handbrake, the rest is fair and square.'

Distracted by the bare-faced lie and stung into fresh indignation, Manningford railed, 'Fair and square my arse. This car is a classic of its time, and I thought that's the sort of thing you were supposed to be specialising in. I've looked after this car. Most of what you've got on this invoice is work I had done in Market Darley not six weeks past.'

'Prove it.'

'What plugs do you stock in this pokey, tuppenny-ha'penny shack, eh? Show me. Go on, show me. Because six weeks ago I ordered the special diamond ones for this, and if they're not still under the bonnet at this very minute I'll eat my hat.'

'I may have overlooked that as well.' Lowry was in retreat.

'Overlooked it? You're a crook, man, and you can overlook just about everything else on this invoice. I'll pay for the oil and not a penny more. You did change the oil, I suppose?'

'Oh, fuck off and take your motor with you. You're all the same, you people with money – long pockets and short arms.'

'And you're all the same, those who can't be bothered to work for it like the rest of us – you think you're entitled to take it from those who have got it. Miss Cadogan was right. You're just like that miserable old git of an uncle of yours.'

'Ah, sod off.'

'And a good morning to you, gentlemen,' Falconer greeted them, strolling on to the forecourt followed by Carmichael (or should that be *Cowmichael* today?) 'Not so fast, Mr Manningford.' Piers was insinuating himself into the driving seat of an immaculate, old T-registration Renault 18 Turbo. 'I shall need to speak to you again. Will you be in if I call in – say, about half an hour?'

'I'll be there.'

'Good-oh! Now, Lowry, shall we go into the shop where there's a modicum of privacy? We wouldn't want to cause a public disturbance now, would we?'

138

V

Lowry, of course, denied any knowledge of a will made by his great-uncle. He also displayed a similar ignorance of any bank account or insurance policy the old man may have had, but he looked happier and happier as the interview continued. So what if he had no alibi for Sunday evening? Having one would have been, in itself, suspicious. They would have to prove he had been in the cottage.

As they left, Carmichael furnished the inspector with his opinion.

'He seemed pretty confident to me, sir. And he genuinely didn't seem to know about the account and the policy.'

'Be that as it may, Carmichael, he'd have known the old man owned the property, and knew or suspected he had a cache of money tucked away somewhere in there. How much do you reckon a place like that would fetch on the open market, even in that state, in a village setting like this? Those two nest eggs together were enough for him to commit murder for. The other two golden eggs are just the icing on the cake. Somehow we've got to place him in that cottage.'

'If it was him.'

'Yes. Now, let's get off and see what Mr Manningford's opinion of blackmail is. Then, when we've shaken his tree a little, we'll go and see what Nicholas Rollason has to say for himself about that missing hour or so of his on Sunday night.'

Chapter Twelve

Wednesday 15th July – morning

I

Falconer decided to leave the car where it was. It was a nice day and he had at least found a parking space. As they passed the teashop, Cassandra Romaine hailed them from the green. She was sitting on the bench by the war memorial, a full wicker shopping basket beside her.

'It's my husband's birthday today,' she trilled, 'and we're having drinkies and nibbles in the pub tonight. Do you fancy joining us?'

'No thank you, Mrs Romaine. I hope you have a good time,' called Falconer loudly, then, dropping his voice, he muttered, 'After all, you are that good time that's been had by just about all. You didn't want to go, did you, Carmichael?'

'No way, sir.'

'Too right. The drinkies may be OK, but as for the nibbles – I'd rather be nibbled by a piranha fish.'

'I don't think I'd fancy either, but it takes all sorts.'

Was that Carmichael making a joke?

II

Piers Manningford was in, and waiting for them. Dorothy was working away for a few days, and he was very glad indeed of her absence. Whatever was to be discussed this morning would include part of his life that he would rather his wife was kept in the dark about. So, although it was with a certain amount of trepidation that he opened the door to the summoning knock, he felt fairly sure that his secret was safe, at least for now.

'Come in, Inspector, come in, Sergeant. Go through and sit down. I've just made a pot of coffee.'

'Nasty business at the garage this morning, sir.' Falconer fired his opening shot.

'It was, it was. But I'm not ashamed at losing my temper. The man was blatantly trying to rip me off.'

'Perfectly within your rights, sir,' the inspector agreed. 'Rather, I was referring to Lowry's rough-shod manner with Miss Cadogan.'

'He's a guttersnipe. I called round after I got home and the little dog's fine, just a bit sore, but she was really upset. Said Buster had had a bad enough time with his old master, and it wasn't fair, him being kicked like that when he'd done nothing wrong.'

'Maybe she'll have the common sense to steer clear of that young man in the future.'

'Let's hope so. Now, how do you take your coffee?'

'Black, no sugar,' instructed Falconer.

'White, five sugars,' requested Carmichael.

Five sugars! That explained a lot, thought Falconer. He took a sip from his cup, placed it on the occasional table beside his chair, and went straight for the jugular. 'Was Reg Morley trying to blackmail you, Mr Manningford?'

An arc of coffee flew from Piers' lips and into his lap as he choked in surprise. Mopping furiously at his groin area, he vigorously denied the allegation.

'What would happen if your wife found out about your little romps with Mrs Romaine?'

Manningford stopped mopping. 'She'd rip me to ribbons verbally, throw everything not nailed down at my head, pack my bags, throw me out, contact her solicitor and launch extremely acrimonious divorce proceedings. That's what would happen. There, does that satisfy you?'

'What would you be willing to pay to keep it quiet?'

'I have very little money of my own.'

'Then what would you be prepared to do to guarantee silence?'

'I don't know what you mean.'

'Of course you do, Mr Manningford. Would you be prepared to commit murder?'

'Don't be absurd.'

'Did Mr Morley try to blackmail you, Mr Manningford?'

'Stop it, stop it! I didn't touch him. He never said anything. I'm not even sure it was him in the woods. Why don't you leave me in peace and try to find out who really did it. You'll destroy me if you carry on like this.' Sweat poured down his face, and his eyes were red and brimming with tears.

'Thank you for the coffee, Mr Manningford. We'll be in touch. Shall we see ourselves out?'

III

The walk to The Rookery to see Nick Rollason would normally have been a waste of time as, on a Wednesday, that gentleman was usually to be found in his office in Carsfold. Today, however, he had found it necessary to return home for some clients' files he had inadvertently left on his desk, and was just collecting these together when the two policemen arrived.

'Come on in, you're lucky to catch me. I'm normally in the office at this time. My wife said you had a chat with her yesterday. How can I help you?'

'Let's start with Sunday afternoon.' Falconer had been directed to an armchair, Carmichael, notebook at the ready, was perched incongruously on a green pouffe, giving the uncanny impression of a mountain placed on a pea. 'Your wife says she heard Ms Long shouting after Mr Morley as he left to walk his dog. Did you hear her too?'

'No. That was when Becky was opening up, and I was out in the back garden mowing the lawn. Daren't leave it at this time of the year, especially after such a wet spring, or the grass is up to your armpits before you know it.'

'Did you see Mr Morley at all on Sunday?'

'Not to my knowledge.'

'Had you been bothered by Mr Morley spying on your wife?'

'Becky and I decided to ignore it. She didn't want any bad feeling between neighbours.'

'So why did you go over to see him on Sunday evening?'

'I didn't.'

'You were seen.'

Nick Rollason sighed. 'OK, pax. I went out to the pub for a couple of pints and had rather more than I intended. I got all worked up about that dirty old man ogling my wife and decided to have a quiet word with him.'

'And did you?' questioned Falconer, expecting a denial.

'Yes, I did. I told him quietly and precisely that if he didn't stop his peeping-tommery immediately, I'd wring his scrawny little neck for him.' Rollason looked very unhappy at this admission and hung his head. 'When I heard what had happened I felt dreadful, as if I'd somehow wished it on him. God knows, I only meant to frighten him, and the next morning he was dead.'

'What time did this take place, sir?'

'I left the pub a few minutes after nine. That's as close as I can get. And the whole thing can't have lasted more than a minute or two.'

Thank you God, thought Falconer, before going for the throat. 'So why did it take you over an hour to get home? It's a distance of only a few yards.'

'I went for a walk to clear my head.'

'You were seen heading towards your own home. Are you sure that wasn't to get a bit of wire from the shed, so that you could return and solve your peeping tom problem once and for all?' This didn't account for the sleeping tablets, but Falconer had

144

to try for whatever he could get.

'Don't be absurd. I'd had too much to drink and I was all steamed up. Yes, I did head towards home, but I decided to keep on going up the High Street and have a tramp around the ruins until I felt calmer and more sober. Then I went home.'

'Do you realise that you might have been the last person to see Mr Morley alive?'

'Very unlikely – in fact it's impossible, Inspector.'

'What makes you say that?'

'Because that would make me a murderer, wouldn't it, and I'm afraid you're going to have to look elsewhere for someone to fill that role.'

'Bugger!' said Falconer as they took their leave. 'Either he's an exceptional actor, or I've just made a bit of a tit of myself.'

'Do you like bird-watching, sir?'

'No, Carmichael.'

After a minute or so, during which both men remained silent, Falconer resumed. 'Let's call at The Old Manor House while we're up this end. I've a feeling I know what that old boy's hiding and I want to put my theory to the test, see if I can't bluff him out into the open.'

'Can I help?' asked Carmichael, eager as a big brown puppy.

'Just go along with anything I say, even if you know I'm lying. And try not to look surprised, OK?'

'OK.'

The Brigadier and his lady wife were taking elevenses in the garden, and the policemen were invited to sit and partake of a cup of Darjeeling and some excellent home-made flapjacks. A plate of scones, a pat of butter and a glass bowl of jam also sat on the table.

'Tell me again,' said Falconer with a light spray of oatmeal, 'when did you go down to Crabapple Cottage on Sunday?'

'Went down about nine. Knocked on the door, called out. Nothing. Heard shouting round the back and decided to call it a day.'

'You didn't speak to Mr Morley at all?'

'No. Told you, couldn't get an answer.'

'But did you speak to him when you went back later?'

'Young man, are you all right?' cut in Joyce Malpas-Graves as Carmichael began to cough convulsively.

'I'm fine,' he managed between splutters. 'Crumb went down the wrong way.'

The Brigadier banged him on the back while his wife passed his cup to him. Falconer merely glared in fury. So much for Carmichael keeping a cool head as he, Falconer, tried to flush out the truth. At the first sign of a bluff, Carmichael nearly chokes to death in surprise. If I were ten years younger, thought the inspector, and two feet taller, I'd give him a proper slap. And not on the back either.

'Brigadier, if I can get back to what we were saying.' Carmichael was silent now, but red in the face from his recent paroxysm. 'You returned to Crabapple Cottage on Sunday evening. You couldn't make yourself heard when you called earlier, so you returned.'

'Who says I went back.'

'You were seen.' (Carmichael was staring innocently into his cup, fully aware of the rules now, and playing the game.)

'Oh.' The Brigadier (trusting soul) deflated a little. 'Fair play, old chap. Yes, I did go back.' (Yippee!)

'What time?'

'About half past nine.'

'And did you speak to Mr Morley?'

'I did.'

'Tell me.'

'I'd better tell you why I went back, first, so it makes more sense. When I got home the first time Joyce was all in a tizzy. This is jam-making season, and while I was out she'd gone to fetch in some gooseberries as she knew we had enough to make a few pounds – so much better than that shop-bought muck. But when she got to the bushes there wasn't a single fruit to be found. Morley had already been at our soft fruits – raspberries, strawberries – and when I realised he'd been at it again I really saw red. Had a quick gin-and-it for Dutch courage and marched back down there. Pushed my way past him and went straight to the kitchen. And there they were – the best part of three and a half pounds of gooseberries in an old carrier bag.'

'What did you do then?'

'Grabbed 'em and told the old sod a thing or two.'

'Don't be modest, sir. What thing or two did you tell him?'

'That he deserved a good thrashing and, if he stole from me again, I'd have him arrested.'

'And that's all?'

'Yes.'

'Did you see anyone on the way home?'

'Too angry to notice if there was anyone about. By the way, who saw me and blabbed?'

'No one, Brigadier. I made that bit up, I'm afraid.'

'Well, I'll be blowed!'

'Would either of you gentlemen like a scone?' Joyce Malpas-Graves offered. 'There's some very nice gooseberry jam to go with them.'

Chapter Thirteen

Wednesday 15th July – afternoon

I

Falconer and Carmichael spent the remains of the working day behind their desks, in the time-consuming pursuit of building a comprehensive case file thus far, pairing signed statements with notes taken, preparing hitherto unsigned information to statement forms, and compiling progress reports. It was tedious but necessary work, and both men ploughed on in comparative silence, merely wishing the task done and the hours to the end of the working day over.

Back in Castle Farthing there were, in most cases, enjoyable preparations afoot for the evening's celebration of Clive Romaine's birthday at The Fisherman's Flies. Paula and George Covington were arranging (and protecting with cling-film) such comestibles as smoked salmon sandwiches (crusts still attached), cheese and broccoli quiches (suitable for vegetarians), sausage rolls (suitable for omnivores), smoked trout goujons with a dill dip, and filled rolls for those requiring more than a mere morsel of sustenance. The dual motivations of a fun evening twinned with excellent profits spurred their creative geniuses, and they sprinkled cress and dealt prettily halved tomatoes with gay abandon, and hoped that their offerings would pass muster with the decidedly unvillagey Romaines.

The Rollasons were collecting together the plethora of equipment and supplies necessary to the passing of an evening for a baby in an unfamiliar household. Little Tristram was to spend the evening in Jasmine Cottage with Kerry Long's children in the care of Rosemary Wilson, who was more than happy to forego the pleasures of an alcohol-fuelled knees-up for the chance to play nanny to three young charges.

And, oh, the choices to be made. Should a spare sleep-suit be included in the little man's baggage? Should she put in his bunny-wunny but leave out the teddy with the sleepy-time eyes? She had better put them both in. The noise from the garage workshop carried in the warm, evening air, and for the last few days Tristram had

149

slept only fitfully until it ceased, which happened far too late in her and her husband's opinion. The poor little chap, usually so happy and contented, was definitely showing signs of fatigue in his sudden tears at the slightest thing. She herself was feeling a little frayed at the edges at the constant running up and down in the evenings to comfort and resettle him.

It was all quiet now, however, and her thoughts drifted back to the task in hand. Would one bottle be sufficient? Better make that two – one of milk and one of juice. Had Nick taken the travel cot over? Where were the spare dummies? How many napkins? Rebecca's head was in a spin as she surveyed the ocean of things she felt would be needed by Tristram to go a-visiting for just a few short hours. All in all, taking into account his full complement of equipment: pram, pushchair, highchair, play pen, walker, and a whole lot of other must-haves for the average toddler these days, he probably had more possessions than his parents.

Across the green, Kerry Long was enjoying a moment of her new-found peace selecting what to wear, and choosing what make-up would enhance her outfit of choice. Freed from the tyranny under which they had lived since moving there, Dean and Kyle were outside in the mercifully dog-dirt-free garden whooping with delight in their imaginings, in the secure knowledge that there would be no yells of complaint across the fence, no more censure of their natural youthful exuberance.

Their mother pulled a lavender T-shirt dress from its hanger and selected a fuchsia pink 'shrug' with a smile. With her old sparring partner removed, and the thought of the money which would secure her regular (and generous, if Uncle Alan's solicitor had anything to do with it) maintenance payments, life looked sweeter than it had since the break-up of her marriage.

II

Down at the vicarage, the Reverend Bertie struck an ungainly attitude on the side of the bath as he attempted to trim his toenails, while his wife stood at the mirror above the wash hand basin doing her best to apply make-up to all of the little canyons that were inexorably changing the familiar landscape of her face, and wondering if anti-wrinkle creams really worked.

'You won't forget you're picking up Aunt Martha, will you?' she asked, the words slightly distorted as she stretched her mouth to apply lipstick.

'I didn't think I was driving tonight. Ungh!' he grunted as a particularly tough piece of nail yielded finally to the clippers.

'Mind out, Bertie. You'll have someone's eye out if you're not careful.'

'Sorry, dearest.'

'And surely you remember what we arranged? You're to take me with you to Auntie's, drop us both off at the pub, bring the car back here, then walk down to join us. It'll save her walking one way, and make sure she gets there. You know how she likes a good old gossip when she gets the chance.'

'Of course I remember now, Lillian,' agreed her

151

long-suffering husband. 'It must be this Morley business that put it out of my head. I'll pick her up as promised. I say, she seems to have recovered well from losing her friend – Evelyn, wasn't it?'

'That's the one. Yes, she has rather bounced back over the past few months, but then at her age she must be getting quite used to outliving her contemporaries. Wasn't it just typical of her to volunteer to nurse her those last few weeks? She's far braver than I am.'

'Nonsense. Cometh the hour and all that. She's just a good, Christian woman who rose to the occasion. They'd known each other for donkeys' years. You'd do the same if it was your old crony Audrey.'

Lillian Swainton-Smythe put down her mascara wand and gazed sightlessly towards her reflection. 'I probably would, Bertie. You're right, as always.'

III

In his bed-sit at the rear of the garage Mike Lowry also looked forward to the evening in his own way. He had not ceased his dawn to dusk work at the rear of his establishment, realising that the injection of cash from his late, unlamented great-uncle was not a fortune of sufficient size on which to rest his laurels. Rather, it was enough to help re-equip his ageing tools and facilities, and allow him to work on his favourite aspect of the job – to whit, the restoration of vehicles just coming into their own as modern classics: early VW Beetles, Morris 'Moggies', Mini Coopers and the like. Thus he had continued to put in as many hours as he had energy (and spares) for since, on his two current babies (no irony intended here, given his neglect of his flesh and blood children), a Mini Cooper in its original racing green and a Messerschmitt bubble car (his ownership of which shall be left shrouded in mystery). He knew he had been a fool to try and dupe Manningford, but the embarrassment that being found out had caused him still rankled.

Work finished for the day, he cleaned up and took stock of the immediate future. He was a man of means now and would have some respect. As for that little tart who'd turned him down then grassed him up, well, he might have some fun making her squirm. What had he got to lose? Dipping his comb into a jar of hair gel, he applied it to his wayward locks in quest of the quintessential quiff.

IV

The Brigadier and his wife were also in fine form and looking forward to a noggin or two. Their precious kitchen garden had lain unmolested for the third day in a row, and life was good. The chickens were laying, the fruit was ripening, vegetables growing steadily. Mother Nature's weed legions were under control and all was well with their world.

V

In The Old School House Martha Cadogan made her culinary preparations for cats and hedgehogs early, recovered now from the unpleasantness that had occurred that morning. Buster, too, should have an early supper, and maybe a late one too, after his ill treatment earlier. He really was a dear little dog, and she had quickly grown accustomed to, and delighted in, his company.

VI

Next door, in The Beehive, the atmosphere was less relaxed. 'Why did you arrange this, Cassie? You know I don't like a fuss. I'd much rather we'd gone for a drink or a meal, just the two of us.'

'How do you expect to fit in to a community if you don't make the effort? This is the perfect opportunity. I've asked everyone we know and a few we don't, for good measure. It's only for a couple of hours. Why don't you just relax for once and try to have a good time. There's no need to be so tight-arsed about drinks and nibbles in the local. After all, it is your birthday.'

'It doesn't feel like it, the way you're railroading me.'

'Lighten up, Clive. Are you frightened you might have fun?'

'You'd know all about that, wouldn't you?'

'What's that supposed to mean?'

'Nothing.'

'Good,' she said, a final punctuation to the conversation. *Whoops! she thought. Better tread warily tonight. It feels like I might be on thin ice here.*

VII

At Pilgrims' Rest on the corner, Piers Manning-ford paced nervously up and down. To go or not to go, that was the question. If news of his and Cas-sandra's affair were to become common gossip, he didn't dare be seen with her. Either they would appear too familiar or too distant. On the other hand, it would look strange if he did not make an appearance. With Dorothy still away (thank God for small mercies) it would look odd if he chose to spend the evening skulking at home by himself. Piers continued his pacing. Why had he ever em-barked on this crazy liaison? Why was life so complicated? He had been a fool and could already feel the hot breath of the hellhounds of destruction at his heels.

VIII

Rosemary Wilson wandered contentedly across the green towards her babysitting duties. Life had seemed brighter these last few days, her burden lighter. No longer would she have to suffer the petty pilfering of that wretched old man and soon, too, his debt to her would be settled. At least she could be assured of that. And Kerry was so much more relaxed, as were the children, now free to play as they pleased: now free to be children. It

155

might be a wicked thing to think, but Castle Farthing was a better place without its crotchetiest male resident and she, for one, missed him not a jot.

She diverted her course slightly to greet Alan and Marian Warren-Browne who were just leaving their property by the side door, obviously en route for The Fisherman's Flies. 'Looking forward to the jollities?' she called as they turned to wait for her.

'Should be a nice evening.' Alan sounded cheerful enough, but a slight anxiety marred his expression and, although dressed for an evening out, Marian looked strained, her eyes tired.

'Are you all right, my dear?' Rosemary asked in some concern.

'Just the tiny shadow of a headache.'

'It's the noise from that damned garage. It never seems to stop these days. That bloody dog's gone, so now we get this.'

'Don't make a fuss, Alan. I've taken something for it and I'm sure I'll be fine.'

'You go and have a nice evening, you two, and you can tell me all about it over a nice cup of tea tomorrow, Marian.' And, with this, Rosemary Wilson took her leave of them and headed towards Jasmine Cottage, content that her evening would consist only of playing with her three young charges.

Chapter Fourteen

Wednesday 15th July – evening

I

Detective Inspector Harry Falconer was preparing for a rather quieter evening, to be spent in the confines of his own home, said home being a substantial, detached 1950s property in a small cul-de-sac on the outskirts of Market Darley, local planning regulations having thus far declined to allow it to be swamped by the sprawl of the new development which mars so many other small towns. The house he owned outright. His father and grandfather had been successful barristers – his father still was – and, although his parents had vociferously protested against their son's choice of career, Falconer stuck by the principle that he preferred to be on the side of those apprehending miscreants and wrong-doers, than on the side of those accepting obscene (in his opinion) amounts of money to twist testimony and employ obscure loopholes and points of law to secure their freedom to re-offend.

His principles had not, however, led him to re-fuse the proceeds of the trust fund that had come his way at the age of twenty-five, and allowed him both to enter the property market, and to build a modest but expertly chosen shares portfolio, thus launching him simultaneously on the stock market. Over the years that lump sum, plus the accumulation of premiums and profits, had led him to his present abode and its very individual style.

The kitchen was an operating theatre of stainless steel. All the rooms were painted in magnolia, the woodwork white. The flooring was the palest beech wood, relieved by the careful placing of vivid rugs. The seating in the sitting room was of cream leather, the furniture in the dining room of metal, glass and sea-grass. Everywhere was minimalist, with the exception of the largest of the downstairs rooms, which he had designated his study. This room alone spoke of the inner Falconer and what fuelled his intellect and imagination, and filled his hours of leisure.

On one of the walls hung a few Monet prints, and two further walls were lined with bookshelves filled with volumes by his favourite authors. Here Sherlock Holmes sat beside Professor Challenger: *A Study in Scarlet, The Hound of the Baskervilles, The Lost World, The Poison Belt*. M. R. James flanked Edgar Allan Poe. *A Journey to the Centre of the Earth* sat near *The Diary of a Nobody, Three Men in a Boat* and *The Portrait of Dorian Grey*. Although normally a meticulously ordered man, Falconer was ruled by no such pettiness of spirit with his books. He knew where to lay his hands on each and every volume.

A baby grand piano nestled in the bay window, a book of comic songs by Tom Lehrer open on its stand at 'The Masochism Tango'. Although a fairly competent pianist, he had been having a little trouble with the right-hand triplets against the mainstream rhythm of the left hand, and intended to put the piece through its paces later, with the aid of the metronome.

On his desk sat a number of textbooks and cassettes devoted to the Greek (modern) language. He had studied, for a while, the classical tongue at school along with Latin. The former, though more or less lost to him now, had prompted an interest in its modern-day equivalent. As he harboured the ambition, at some point, to indulge in a little flotilla sailing around some of the lesser-frequented Greek islands, a knowledge of the language seemed like a good idea, and was proving an excellent intellectual challenge.

The only other occupant of the house, and Falconer's only (and preferred) company was a seal point Siamese cat, named Mycroft in tribute to the first great (if fictitious) detective's brother.

Falconer had dined well on a fillet steak, chargrilled vegetables with couscous, and a vinaigrette-dressed green salad, Mycroft on a little poached salmon (all bones most carefully removed). Putting their few dishes into the dishwasher, master and cat retired to the study, the former settling purposefully at the piano, the latter on the black, leather swivel chair at the desk. Almost immediately the strains of the introduction to the aforementioned tongue-in-cheek tango rang out, to be joined, at the appropriate point, by a light, but pleasing voice, as the song began. Mycroft purred along in contentment at the sound of his master's voice.

II

Things did not run with such tranquil order in the overcrowded Carmichael household, where the rules were few and simple. If you wanted clean clothes that fitted, get up early. If you wanted to sit down, clear a chair. If you wanted to eat, clear a space at the table, but be sure to be fast in the kitchen before everything went. Mealtimes were not occasions for civilised conversation round the dining table, a piece of furniture that lived in the kitchen and was currently covered in half-empty sauce bottles and food-encrusted plates, with an empty milk bottle perched precariously near the edge, a bluebottle lazily pacing its rim. No, here mealtimes were a battleground; first, to obtain food on whatever assortment of crockery was fit for use and, secondly, to secure somewhere other than the floor to eat it.

Carmichael, a few years ago, had despaired of any sort of order in his daily round and, with the object of remedying this situation, had set to work, with those of his cronies at that time employed in the building trade, on the conversion of a large, brick, shed-like appendage to the property, reached, via a make-shift covered porch, from the kitchen.

Within six months he and his helpers had weatherproofed it, repaired one window and added another. The walls had been given an inner skin of plasterboard and painted, the door replaced with a sturdier model with a Yale lock, this last rescued triumphantly from the local tip.

160

At this point, its new occupant had removed all that he felt he possessed outright from the bedroom he had been sharing with two brothers and moved, as it were, into his own private wing of Carmichael Towers.

Although the furnishings and ornamentation were a somewhat eclectic mix, his den was clean, tidy, and loved. Above all, it offered him the privacy he craved – sanctuary from the slovenly ways of the rest of the household – and was treasured as much by Carmichael as Falconer treasured the somewhat more sumptuous and lavishly appointed establishment that he called home. Carmichael knew about make-do and mend, and the importance of having one's own space, and this went no little way to explain why he had felt such admiration for Kerry Long and her carefully nurtured home.

At seven-thirty that evening, as Falconer began his piano practice, and as the residents of Castle Farthing began to make their separate and several ways to The Fisherman's Flies, Carmichael entered his own private haven carrying a tray on which rested three microwave meals for one (he was, after all, a big lad), six slices of bread and butter, a pint mug of tea (only four sugars in this beverage), and that day's copy of *The Sun*. He too would be having a quiet evening at home.

Chapter Fifteen

Wednesday 15th July – evening

I

All of those asked had taken up the invitation to attend Clive Romaine's birthday celebrations and by eight o'clock, to use the vernacular, the joint was heaving. Trade at the bar was brisk, the food was receiving an enthusiastic reception, and muzak from a number of unobtrusive speakers added to the volume of conversation broken, now and then, with a guffaw of good-natured laughter. As the evening wore on and drink flowed more freely, however, there were to be a number of unpleasant exchanges, some jarring notes amidst the jars of ale.

The first of these occurred shortly after nine o'clock when Nick Rollason, already proved to be an individual more likely to air a grievance after a bevy or two, buttonholed Mike Lowry about the amount of noise that had come from his workshop over the past few evenings.

'I can understand you have a job to do, and I don't begrudge you that, but do you have to carry on till all hours? Some of us have got young children trying to get some sleep, and if you don't do something about it, I shall have to get in touch with the noise abatement people, see what they

162

have to say about it.'

'We can't all work in a poncy office, Rollason. Some of us have to get our hands dirty. Not all of us have nice, clean, quiet jobs shuffling a few bits of paper around.'

'That doesn't answer my question, Lowry. When are you going to let us have a bit of peace and quiet in the evenings?'

'Hear, hear,' cut in Alan Warren-Browne. 'I thought my wife was going to get a respite from her crippling migraines when your uncle's dog went – no offence meant, Miss Cadogan.'

'None taken, Alan.'

'But, oh no. Like a family trait it is, you, him and noise.'

'I can't help it if your old lady's a hypochondriac.'

'She is not.'

'Nor if your kid doesn't want to be poked off to its cot at every opportunity.'

'How dare you!' This last from Rebecca Rollason, crimson with rage.

At this point George Covington lumbered over and steered Mike Lowry towards a darts match in noisy progress at the other end of the bar, his wife in his wake carrying plates of food to offer to those left standing on the still-smouldering battlefield.

Things settled down for a while then, the mechanic tossing arrows towards their circular target, and beer down his throat. The Reverend Bertie Swainton-Smythe, seeing the glasses of his wife and her aunt empty and taking advantage of a lull in activity at the bar, moved to replenish

163

their drinks, almost stumbling to his knees as he attempted to ease himself round the table.

'Watch out, Bertie,' called Lillian, as he grabbed at the bench for balance.

'I'm awfully sorry, Aunt Martha. I seem to have trodden on your handbag.'

'I'm sure there's no harm done. Here, let me put it up on this chair, out of the way.'

'Oh, Auntie! Why didn't you bring something a little more appropriate for the evening?' Lillian was aghast at her aunt's shopping-sized bag.

'Because I stopped having pretty little bags for evenings forty years ago, Lillian. This is my all-occasion, never-have-to-repack-it, never-go-out-without-something bag. Like it or lump it.'

'Aunt Martha, don't tease so. I can see the twinkle in your eye.'

'There's room for that in my bag, too, should I choose to keep it there. There you are, Bertie! Thank you very much. You must let me get the next one. Here's mud in your eye.'

The good-natured atmosphere in the bar pre-vailed for another three-quarters of an hour, during which time heavy rain began to fall from the cloud cover that had stealthily thickened as daylight had faded. Martha Cadogan, true to her word, had taken her humongous handbag to the bar to order a round of drinks, and was a reluctant close witness to what happened next.

Mike Lowry had continued to drink steadily and to walk a little less so. On one of his not infrequent trips from the bar he cannoned into Brigadier Malpas-Graves, as the older man collected two pink gins for himself and his wife. 'Steady on, old man. Plenty of time till closing,' he warned.

'Ah, if it isn't the Brigadier. Sir,' he said, putting his pint down on a table. A dangerous glint had appeared in the mechanic's eye and he seemed bent on making mischief, 'I believe I owe you a great big thank you.'

'What for, my boy?'

'From what I've gathered, it was you that did away with my tight-fisted old Great-uncle Reg. What a favour that was. Perhaps I ought to buy you a drink, in gratitude, shall we say.'

'Whatever are you talking about, man? Explain yourself.'

'You went down to his place Sunday night, didn't you?'

'I think you'd better keep your accusations to yourself, young man, or you'll be hearing from my solicitor.'

'But I'm only trying to say thank you, aren't I? For finding me a fortune, although anyone less like Chris Tarrant I'd be hard pressed to find,' this reference to *Who Wants To Be A Millionaire?* being a complete mystery to the Brigadier.

'You leave him alone, Mike, and stop shooting your mouth off. You'll get into all sorts of trouble if you're not careful.' Mike turned to the source of these words: his erstwhile partner, Kerry Long.

'Oh, if it isn't the money-grubbing bitch who makes my life a misery with her whining. Frightened he'll take me to court and you'll lose your precious maintenance, are you?'

'Calm down. Let's all calm down. This is supposed to be a birthday party.' Clive Romaine stepped in to try his hand at peace-making, but to no avail.

'Well, if it isn't the husband of the local bicycle. What's it like not knowing who's been in your wife's knickers from day to day?'

'What the hell are you implying?'

'Leave it, Clive.' Cassandra tried to pull her husband away.

Lowry, at that moment, caught sight of Piers Manningford's face, thought he saw the way the wind was blowing, and decided to get his own back for his earlier humiliation on his own forecourt. Maybe it was his turn to get caught with his trousers down. 'Oh, I thought better of it. Didn't know where it had been. But ask that next-door neighbour of yours. He'll give you chapter and verse on her cheap favours, if I'm not very much mistaken.'

'What's he talking about, Cassie?'

'Nothing. Leave it. He's drunk, that's all.'

The Reverend Bertie hove into view from one direction at that juncture, while George Covington appeared from the other. 'Come along, Michael. Let's get you home,' said the vicar, brooking no argument. 'You restore order with the others, George. Leave this one to me. Now, where's your glass?' Bertie handed him his glass. 'Now, get that down you and I'll see you home.'

The application of a little more ale seemed to have a pacifying effect on Lowry, for he became almost meek, allowing himself to be seen safely back to his bed-sit, from where he could do no further mischief that evening, and the vicar left him, in an armchair, eyes already closing in sleep.

As he stepped back over to the pub he noticed

that there had been a temporary respite from the rain, but thunder now rumbled ominously in the distance, promising more to come, and lightning flickered intermittently in the west.

The party was breaking up on his return, there being too many ruffled feathers to maintain even the illusion of a congenial social gathering, and each went their separate ways to evaluate and think on what the evening's events meant to them.

At eleven-forty-five the thunder and lightning were directly over the village of Castle Farthing and a deluge of rain began to fall.

All but one of its residents listened in awe as the summer storm raged.

II

Castle Farthing was not, however, abed for the night, as could be seen in the bright lightning flashes that intermittently bathed it in an eerie blue light. During this time, in one of Mother Nature's flickering slide shows, an observer would have noticed a dark figure flitting along the Carsfold Road. A few minutes earlier, the first figure to venture out had left a property on the High Street and disappeared into the storm. Over a period of a few minutes two more figures braved the elements. After about five minutes a final figure left the comforts of hearth and home and disappeared into the dark, rain-lashed night.

None was abroad for pleasure

Chapter Sixteen

Thursday 16th July – morning

I

Harry Falconer had, unusually and infuriatingly, slept through the summons of his alarm clock and emerged dripping and late from his shower to discover that he had a dozen clean shirts, but not one had been ironed. It was, therefore, with a hiss of exasperation that he dug out the ironing board, made hasty work of a cream linen number, and threw on his clothes.

Mycroft had the unexpectedly dull breakfast of tinned cat food shoved unceremoniously under his nose, and was deciding to turn said nose up in disdain when his master fled through the front door muttering curses under his breath. The cat, defeated, gave the feline equivalent of a sigh and moodily tucked in. Without an audience, no display of petulance would change the menu, and food, after all, was food – in fact, not bad at all for tinned, but he would not be letting on about that, just in case.

His master's day did not improve when, on arriving at his desk, he shed his jacket to make an awful discovery. In his haste earlier, he must have been so distracted as to have ironed one of his shirt sleeves twice, the other, not at all. His left arm was draped from shoulder to cuff in wrinkled cream linen. That was just grand! He would have to spend the whole of today with his jacket on. But at least the previous night's storm had cleared the air a little and it was somewhat cooler today.

As he sneeringly contemplated the scar on his normal sartorial perfection, the internal telephone trilled for attention and he reached to answer it, still glaring in disbelief at his left arm.

'Great. Super. Oh, marvellous. Straight away?' There went the last vestige of the idea that he might be able to slip home and press the offending sleeve. 'Carmichael's waiting to be picked up. Oh, goody. I'm on my way.'

Another body had been discovered in Castle Farthing and their urgent presence was requested. There had been no other details except the fact that one Constable Proudfoot would be found on duty, guarding the remains and whatever evidence there may be.

II

Carmichael had indeed bowed to the dictates of a lower temperature and had, in part at least, fulfilled the unspoken wishes of his superior. He was wearing long trousers, a tie, and a shirt, and the shirt was even long-sleeved and white. Unfortunately the trousers were of a bright crimson material and made his gangling legs look as if he had severed both femoral arteries simultaneously. His tie, Falconer noticed with dismay, carried a likeness of the cartoon character Taz the Tas-

169

manian Devil attempting to devour a cartoon rabbit which was parachuting slowly (he guessed) towards the waiting, gaping mouth. Falconer sighed a weary sigh. Why didn't the man just hire a Batman costume and have done with it? At least that would be recognisable as fancy dress.

From over his shoulder Carmichael pulled a vivid green jacket, and folded it into his lap as he shimmied into the passenger seat. Red and green! Make that Robin, thought Falconer, but then, perhaps not: that would make *him* Batman. He then remembered the state of his own shirt, blushed very slightly and drove off, trying to focus his attention on the case thus far.

III

They found Constable Proudfoot on the forecourt of the Castle Farthing Garage in Drovers Lane, the area to the rear of the pumps already taped off and out of bounds to any other than the official players in this drama.

'Is it Lowry?' Falconer asked without salutation or preamble.

'Yes, sir. It's young Lowry.'

'Murder?'

'Definitely. Looks the same as the last one to me.'

'Thank you, Proudfoot. I didn't ask for your opinion. I'll make my own mind up, if I may. Who found him?'

'Mr Warren-Browne from the post office.'

'Again?'

170

'Again. Bit unlucky that, really, finding two dead bodies in less than a week.'

'Unlucky is one word for it. Let's hope he doesn't make a habit of it. Anyone in there at the moment – police surgeon, scenes-of-crime?'

'Just the vicar.'

'Dear God and all the saints, don't tell me you've let the vicar in again? What kind of a moron are you, Proudfoot? You'll be selling tickets next and letting in parties of pensioners, half price, to have a little dust round and a tidy-up. Get out of my way, man, before I do something really unprofessional.'

The inspector pushed his way under the tape and marched towards the rear of the garage. Carmichael, mightily amused, winked at the blushing constable and resisted the urge to limbo under the tape in pursuit of his superior.

As the acting sergeant reached the door of the bed-sit, a familiar tableau greeted his eyes. An obviously dead body lay slumped in an armchair, Rev. Bertie Swainton-Smythe was just scrambling from his knees before it, and Falconer was in full flow. 'This is déjà-bloody-vu isn't it, vicar. Tell me, if there's ever a third body, will I be treated to the unusual experience of déjà-bloody-vu all over again?'

'I'm sorry, Inspector. Marian Warren-Browne phoned me as soon as Alan got back to the post office and phoned 999. I know you've got a job to do, but so have I, and this is it. Shall I turn out my pockets now?'

'Please.'

He produced a bunch of keys, a crumpled

171

handkerchief and an assortment of small change.

'Thank you. Now go. Carry on praying if you must, but do it somewhere else and stop muddying the forensic evidence. Get out. I'll be along to see you later.'

Left to themselves Falconer and Carmichael surveyed the living accommodation of the recently deceased. It did not amount to much. A sofa bed at the far side of the room had not been folded away since its last use, and the sheets and quilt lay crumpled across it. A cumbersome old television set rested on a low, dark wood table, a small bookcase held car maintenance manuals and a few 'top shelf' magazines. There were no pictures on the walls save for a calendar for a bygone year showing scantily clad females, a good-will offering from a well-known tyre company. One corner housed a sink and portable gas ring, an alcove next to this, a none-too-clean lavatory and minute shower with a mould-encrusted curtain.

The only armchair housed the mortal remains of Michael Lowry, great-nephew and only living adult relative of the late and unlamented Reginald Morley. Much good his inheritance had done him!

His fate appeared to have been much the same as old Great-uncle Reg's, too. His face was a swollen gargoyle, and there were signs of a ligature buried in the skin of his neck. No signs of any cocoa, but Falconer would put his shirt (he winced) on there being diazepam in the young man's stomach.

Turning to his sergeant, he found him lost in a brown study. 'What's on your mind, Carmichael?'

172

'I was just thinking what a pity it all was, for him to end up like this. He had it all going for him really – good-looking chap like that and now with money coming his way. Still, he was a shit to his wife and kids – excuse the language, sir. I dunno, seems a waste though.'

Falconer turned on his heel and left the bed-sit. Carmichael in thoughtful mood was more than he felt up to coping with just at the moment.

IV

The post office was the obvious starting point for them. They would glean what information they could on the discovery of the body, then try to work their way backwards in time. Had there not been some sort of a 'do' at the local pub the night before? Maybe Lowry had gone to that. After the post office they would make a quick trip there to see what the landlord and his good lady had to offer.

Once more Alan Warren-Browne looked grey about the gills when he bade them enter and follow him, for the second time in three days, up-stairs to the chintzy sitting room above his work premises. This time, however, Marian Warren-Browne was present and sitting in an armchair drinking a cup of tea (coffee aggravated her migraine) and reading a magazine.

Seeing them enter, she disappeared into the kitchen. Returning with two cups and saucers, she poured for them and watched the contents of the sugar bowl decrease alarmingly as Car-

173

michael adjusted the brew to his particular taste.

'I seem to be making a habit of this, don't I, Inspector?'

'You do indeed, Mr Warren-Browne. Would you care to tell me exactly how you discovered this body?' (You're not collecting them for some sort of badge, are you? thought Falconer silently.)

'I'd promised Marian I'd pop into the supermarket in Carsfold for some bulk stuff for the freezer. Thought I'd go in early so I could be back in time to open up. The supermarket opens at eight, so I left about twenty to, only to find that I was virtually out of petrol. But that wasn't a problem, because Lowry was normally up and about by seven-thirty, and perfectly happy to take money off any early customers who stopped by on the off chance.

'So I drove on to the forecourt, but couldn't see him. I waited a minute, then got out of the car to see if he was around. The shop had no light on and was showing a closed sign, so I thought I'd try round the back. Couldn't find him out there either, then I remembered how drunk he'd been the night before and wondered if he was suffering from a bit of a hangover. Hoped he was, actually.'

'How did you know he was drunk the previous night?'

'Everyone was over at the pub for Clive Romaine's birthday. And Mike certainly made sure that everyone knew he was there. Had words with just about everyone, he did.

'But back to this morning. I looked through the window – he doesn't bother with curtains, the glass is dirty enough to give some privacy – and I

174

could see him in that armchair, spark out, as I thought then. I tapped on the window – no response, so I rapped on the door. By then I was impatient to be on my way, so that I could be back in time to open up, so I tried the door and it wasn't locked. And there he was, and now I shall have to go shopping this evening instead.'

Callous bastard, thought Falconer, then returned to an earlier point in the post-master's monologue. 'Did he have words with you?'

'What?'

'Mike Lowry. Were you one of the people he had words with in the pub yesterday evening?'

'We had a slight falling out over the amount of noise that had been coming from his workshop, but it was mostly bluster and the drink talking, I realised. He probably wouldn't even have remembered it, the way he was stumbling around when the vicar took him home.'

'The vicar took him home?'

'That's right. Seemed the best thing to do, and the party broke up shortly after that.'

The vicar again, thought Falconer, but would not let himself be side-tracked. 'What time did you retire last night?'

Marian answered. 'I went to bed about eleven and took a sleeping tablet.'

'And you, sir?'

'Stopped up to watch a film. Didn't notice the time when I finally turned in.'

'Did you notice it, Mrs Warren-Browne?'

'I told you, I'd taken a sleeping tablet.' And with this evasive answer they had to be content for the time being.

As they left by the side door, Falconer said just three words. 'Vicarage, Carmichael. Now.'

V

Lillian Swainton-Smythe admitted them. 'Good morning, Inspector. Ah, I see you still have Ronald MacDonald with you. Do come through, we're in the sun lounge,' this last proving to be a rickety lean-to affair attached precariously to the south-facing wall of the vicarage. 'Bertie, the police to see you. Again.' Surely she could not have been drinking at this early hour? 'Can I take your jacket, Inspector? It's rather warm out there.'

'No thank you,' Falconer replied, once more conscious of the disgraceful condition of his left shirt sleeve. He'd just have to sweat it out.

'Good morning again, Inspector, Sergeant,' the vicar greeted them.

'Why didn't you tell us you'd taken Lowry home from the pub last night?' Falconer was prickly with more than just heat.

'You didn't give me much of a chance to tell you anything, as I remember,' replied the vicar, still smarting from their peremptory treatment of him earlier.

'Shall I turn out my pockets for you, Inspector, or would you like to conduct a body search?' Lillian leered, leaning close to him, the unmistakable smell of gin on her breath.

'Go and lie down, Lillian. You're upset.'

Unexpectedly, she complied, and wandered from their company and into the main body of

176

the vicarage.

'Sorry about that. She's highly strung,' explained Bertie. It seemed a little more tactful than describing her as 'tight', and he was, overall, a tactful man who tolerated and overlooked his wife's occasional little lapses.

'Perhaps you'd tell us about last night, sir? Why did you need to escort Mr Lowry home?'

'There'd been words. He'd upset a few people. I wasn't really listening, then things got rather louder and I felt it my Christian duty to try to pour oil on troubled waters.'

'And what happened?'

'Not a lot. I just stepped in to distract him while George Covington, the landlord, drew attention back to the party. I told him he'd had enough, passed him his pint then, when he'd drunk it, I took him over to his bed-sit.'

'What condition did you consider him to be in?'

'Pretty far gone. He was stumbling all over the place when we got to his door. I had to prop him up against the wall and get his key out of his pocket myself before I could get him inside. By the time I'd manhandled him into the chair he was just about incoherent, and started to snore almost immediately. I had no chance of moving him on my own if he was out cold – he was a dead weight. Oh, my dear Lord, what an unfortunate choice of phrase. I do apologise. Anyway, I thought it was best just to leave him where he was until he came round in his own good time – except that he didn't, did he?'

'Sadly, no. Now, did you lock the door before

you left?'

'I couldn't. You may not have noticed, but there's no Yale lock on that door, only a mortise, and it doesn't have a letterbox. All his post goes – sorry, *went* – to the shop. I could hardly lock him in and put the key through the shop door. There isn't an interconnecting door between the two, as that bed-sit's really just a part of the workshop roughly converted. I just slipped the key back in his pocket and closed the door behind me. May God forgive me!' he expostulated. 'If I could have locked that door he might still be alive. I left that door unlocked for a murderer.' The vicar's face was stricken and drained of all colour.

'Don't distress yourself, sir. If someone is determined to do murder, they'll find a way. You are in no respect responsible for what happened later.'

'I must pray for forgiveness.'

'Before you do that, sir, can you tell me if you recognise these names?' Falconer had produced a small piece of paper from his jacket's inner pocket. 'John and Catherine Marchant,' he read. 'They were witnesses to the will, made about ten years ago, that we found in Mr Morley's cottage.'

Momentarily curbed in his flight to seek forgiveness, Rev. Bertie wrinkled his brow and thought. 'No. Yes. Yes, now I remember. They ran The Fisherman's Flies for a few months as temporary managers, just about the time that Lillian and I moved to this parish, but I haven't the foggiest idea where they are now. Perhaps the brewery might have a record of them.'

'Thank you very much, sir. We'll see ourselves out, shall we?'

178

When Falconer had pulled the piece of paper from his pocket, he had become aware of another object and, as they left the vicarage, fished it out and glanced at it, before slipping it back into his right-hand outer jacket pocket. It was the odd coin that Carmichael had picked up in Reg Morley's back garden. He'd not worn that jacket since Monday, and had forgotten it was there. He must remember to find out what it was and lodge it with all the other flotsam and jetsam of the case.

Falconer did not speak again until they were headed along Church Street towards the green. 'Pub next, I think. That landlord is a pretty shrewd fellow, and his wife's a bit of a smart cookie too. Whatever went on in that pub last night, between them, they'll have it, chapter and verse.'

Chapter Seventeen

Thursday 16th July – morning

I

The Fisherman's Flies was not yet open for business and George Covington had to draw the heavy bolts on one half of the double doors to admit them. He greeted them with the words, 'Grim business, this. Anything we can do to help, we will.' Then he called over his shoulder to his wife. 'Paula, love. Police. Do us a tray.'

The bar smelled as all bars do when closed.

There was the sour tang of stale beer in the air, the smell of stale cooking, and the acrid reek that a place exudes when it has absorbed the smoke from countless cigarettes over a great many years, a reek that persisted even though smoking had now been relegated to the beer garden by the government ban. It was a depressing smell, totally different from that given off by a bar open to, and peopled by, its customers.

The three men had just seated themselves at one of the tables when Paula Covington pushed her way through from behind the bar. She carried a tray on which squatted four cups of individual filter coffee, the liquid still dripping through the fragrant grounds as she set one before each of them and, retaining the fourth for herself, sat down to join them.

'What happened to him, Inspector?' she asked, not at all shy of appearing nosy. 'Was it the same as the old man, or was it an accident of some sort? Lots of dangerous machinery in a garage, especially when you're three sheets to the wind.'

'It was no accident, Mrs Covington, but I'd rather not go into details just at the moment.' He wouldn't need to and he knew it. The village grapevine would soon see to that.

'We understand,' Falconer continued, 'that there was a party here last night, during the course of which there was some unpleasantness involving Mr Lowry. Would you care to tell us anything you can remember?'

George Covington was the first to offer his recollection of events. 'There was a bit of a to-do early on. Young Lowry had been working to all

180

hours out back in his workshop, and sound does carry in a quiet little backwater like this.'

'We didn't tend to notice it in the evenin', what wiv the noise in the bar,' Paula added. 'But it's been goin' on long after we've shut up shop.'

'That's right.' Her husband took over the tale. 'It was young Nick – Nick Rollason – that started it. He's normally very quiet, but he can get a bit bolshie with a few beers inside him. He'd told Lowry to keep it down a bit as it was keeping his kid awake.'

'What was Lowry's reaction to this?'

'Not over co-operative would be a good description.'

'What happened next?'

'Alan from the post office spoke up to defend Nick. The noise was bringing on his wife's migraines again, and he was fair ticked-off about the disturbance.'

'And Mr Lowry's reaction?'

Paula couldn't keep out of it any longer. 'Downright abusive. He accused Marian of swingin' the lead, and the Rollasons of more or less neglectin' that lovely little baby of theirs. Why, they dote on little Tristram – spoil him somethin' rotten. That's when George went over to settle things down.'

'That's right. I sent him off to play darts with some of the local lads, keep him out of mischief for a while.'

'Then it all started up again about ten,' added his wife.

'I only caught the end of that, though.'

'That's right, George, so you did.'

'Was this with the same people?' asked Falconer, eager to cut down his list of runners for the Murder Handicap Chase (the handicap being that he did not, as yet, have a clue who was responsible for either death).

'Glory be, no. Wiv a whole bunch o' new ones. He accused the Brigadier of murderin' his old uncle,' (she counted Lowry's victims off on her fingers) 'poor Kerry of being – what did he call her? – a "money-grubbin' bitch",' she smiled as she recalled the exact wording, 'Clive Romaine – birthday boy for the evenin', God 'elp 'im – of bein' a ... what's that word I want, George? Begins with a 'k' sound.'

'Cuckold.'

'That's it. Never could get the 'ang o' fancy words like that, me. Then 'e more or less called Clive's wife a whore and said she was 'avin' it off wiv that Piers Manningford.'

'That's when I stepped in. Things seemed to be getting a bit out of hand, like, and something had to be done before they got any worse,' said George.

'The vicar offered to take him home?'

'That's right. And just as well. By the time he'd supped his last he could hardly keep upright.'

'Thank you both. Now, was there anything else you remember that might prove useful, before or after closing time?'

'Most of them had gone by half past ten. We shut up at eleven just gone.'

'And that was it?' Falconer had an irresistible urge to push just a bit further.

'I went straight to bed and left George down here to clear up.'

182

'What time did you retire, Mr Covington?'

Suddenly the big man was unsure of himself. 'Can't really remember. Not important, is it?'

'Who knows what may be important. Can you remember what time your husband came up to bed, Mrs Covington?'

'Must've been dead to the world. Didn't know a thing till the alarm went off this mornin'.' But she looked away as she said this last.

II

Their next visit took Falconer and Carmichael to The Rookery where, unexpectedly, they found all three Rollasons. Carmichael had pointed out, as they passed it, that the Castle Farthing Teashop was closed, its doors locked, gingham curtains closed. No tables and chairs sat invitingly out-side, no smells of baking wafted enticingly from its premises.

It was Nick who answered the door to them, his face set in an angry frown. Bidding them enter, he led them to a sitting room strewn with baby toys, around which Tristram toddled, using the furn-iture to keep his balance and pull himself on to greater achievements in his fairly new skill of walking. Occasionally he would stop, grab at a toy, examine it, shake it, and give it an experimental chew before hurling it to the floor with a happy shriek and resuming his dogged circumnavigation.

Rebecca sat on the sofa, her feet drawn up under her, a box of tissues by her side. Her eyes and nose were red and swollen, her hair un-brushed. She looked a picture of misery, managing little more than a wan smile in greeting.

'Do you see what that scum has done to my wife with his filthy, slanderous accusations? She's been breaking her heart that anyone could even think such a thing about us, let alone broadcast it to half the village.'

'I gather you're referring to Mr Lowry and last night's little performance in the pub.'

'Too right I am. I guessed you must have heard about it, when I answered the door to you. There's no sewer that filth flows through quicker than a village.'

'I'm sure you're right, sir,' agreed Falconer, 'but that's not the only reason we've called here.'

'No? Oh, surely it's not about the murder of that old man again? We've said our piece on that and we've absolutely nothing to add. Except, maybe, that that scum of a nephew of his is made in the same mould.'

'Was made,' Falconer hinted.

'I beg your pardon?'

'Past tense, Mr Rollason. I'm afraid that Mr Lowry was murdered last night, sometime after he was seen home after his outbursts in the pub.'

'Oh, no!' Rebecca cried. 'That's awful,' and she began to sob again.

'Don't be so soft, Becky. That one's no loss to anyone. Couldn't have happened to a more deserving chap.'

'You don't mean that, Nick.'

Her husband had the grace to look shame-faced. 'No, I don't suppose I do, but I shan't be shedding any crocodile tears over him, that's for

184

sure. He was a nasty piece of work all round.'

'Yes, but that doesn't mean he deserved to die.'

Falconer and Carmichael left them to it. 'Perhaps not, but he is dead, so the inspector says, and nothing's going to change that. So, good riddance, I say. I'll not be a hypocrite for anyone.'

'Nick, his poor little kiddies.'

'Will be a sight better off without him, so don't be so sentimental. Times will be a lot easier for Kerry and her two, with him out of the way.'

'If I may intervene,' cut in Falconer, who felt he had given them enough free rein to establish their sympathy (or lack of it). 'Would you tell me exactly what time you left the party yesterday evening, and what you did after that?'

'We left straight away, after Lowry implied we were neglectful parents. Becky was distraught and we went straight over to collect Tristram from Rosemary, who was babysitting him at Kerry's cottage along with Kerry's two.'

'Little angel,' cooed Tristram's mother, wiping her eyes and brightening a little. 'He was fast asleep in his travel cot. When I picked him up he gave me such a smile, put his darling little arms round my neck, said "mama" and went straight back to sleep with his head on my shoulder.' The tears returned in an unexpected rush. 'I'm not a bad mother and no one can say I am. I'd die for Tristram. I love him so much it hurts.' Here she broke off and sobbed.

'There, there, love. No one took any notice. Everyone knows you dote on him. We both do. It was only the drink talking, and he's hardly likely to say anything else now, is he?'

185

'Nick!'

'I'm sorry.'

'Mr Rollason, if you wouldn't mind continuing with what happened last night?'

'Of course. Becky carried the little man home and settled him in his cot while I ferried over his equipment – travel cot, toys, bottles, you know. That was it really.'

'What time did you turn in for the night?'

'Becky went straight to bed when Tristram was settled. Cried herself to sleep. She was completely exhausted.'

'And what time did you join her?'

There was a pause. 'I really can't say, you know. I sat down here brooding for a bit, then I had a look at the paper, tried the crossword, but didn't get very far. Must've been pretty late. And we were both shattered this morning, so we decided to spend a few quiet hours at home to recover.'

'Did you notice what time your husband came to bed, Mrs Rollason?'

'I was so worn out with crying I slept like the dead – oh, that poor man,' and two more tears coursed down her already flushed cheeks.

III

As they made their way round the corner towards Pilgrims' Rest, Falconer could not help but express his puzzlement about one aspect of the previous evening. 'What's all this shiftiness about when people went to bed last night?' he asked of Carmichael irritably. The inspector was sweating

186

due to the necessity of keeping his jacket on and the rise in temperature since they had arrived in Castle Farthing earlier that morning. His whole body was overheated and itchy, and he felt sure he was coming out in a heat rash.

'Couldn't say, sir.'

'There's something going on here and I wonder just how widespread it is. I mean, it's hardly likely there was a hole in the space-time continuum and they all got sucked in, is it?'

'In the what, sir?'

'Never mind.'

IV

When Piers Manningford opened the door to them he was a sickly grey colour, he had bags under his eyes and looked like he had hardly slept. 'What do you want?' was his brusque greeting.

'I presume you've heard about Mr Lowry?' Falconer asked.

'What? Shooting his mouth off in the pub about me and Cassie? I was there; I didn't need to hear about it.'

'You've not been out this morning?'

'Do I look as if I'm fit to be seen in public?'

Treating this as a rhetorical question, Falconer announced baldly. 'Mr Lowry is dead.'

'Dead? He can't be! How? Didn't choke on his own bile did he? That'd be poetic justice.'

'Mr Lowry was murdered sometime after leaving the local pub last night.'

'Murdered? Good God, you've not come here

187

to try to pin this on me, have you? For if you have, I want my solicitor present.'

'We've come here to ask you a few questions, that's all, and if you'll let us in, we can conduct this a little less publicly.'

There was no offer of coffee this time, and the sitting room had become dusty and untidy during Dorothy Manningford's absence. Her husband obviously had more on his mind than where the dusters and vacuum cleaner lived.

'Would you tell us, in your own words, what occurred yesterday evening in The Fisherman's Flies, and what you did afterwards, sir?' God! thought Falconer, what a stupid question – who else's words would the man use? And what an opportunity he, himself, had missed. If only he had taken up that invitation to the party from Cassandra Romaine, he could have been in at the kill, as it were. Mentally kicking himself with the boot of hindsight for missing out on such a golden opportunity, he cast a glance at Carmichael to see that he was ready to take notes.

Carmichael was alternately sucking the end of his pen and shaking it. 'What's up?' Falconer hissed.

'Run out, sir.'

'Here, take mine.' Falconer drew an exquisite silver ballpoint pen from his jacket pocket and handed it over. 'And don't suck the end.' Really, with Carmichael around, every day was a circus – the sergeant was certainly dressed like a clown, and now he was acting like one, and making a monkey out of his superior officer to boot.

'I'm sorry about that, sir.' He said to Man-

188

ningford. 'Would you care to start?'

'If you two have finished playing pass the parcel, certainly.' (Ouch!) 'That miserable worm – and no, I'm not sorry he's dead – only went and announced to the whole pub that Cassie and I were having an affair. God, I was scared when I thought old Morley'd seen us, thought he'd either spread it about or bleed me white, or both. Then he was dead and I felt safe again. Then I find out that that old bird next door had sussed us and told you. Martha's OK – I didn't think she'd gossip because of Cassie's kids, but then I had you two to worry about. Jesus, was I glad Dorothy was away. And now this – blown wide open. I've not slept a wink. Someone in this festering hellhole of tittle-tattle is going to see it as their moral duty to inform my wife of 'her husband's adulterous behaviour' and that'll be the end of me. Finito. Ruined.'

'If we could just get back to last night, sir?'

'What? Oh, I came straight home with a sick headache, as you can probably imagine.'

'What time did you go to bed?'

With hardly a hesitation he answered, 'As soon as I'd downed several large scotches and some painkillers. Dorothy's due back this afternoon and I still don't know what the hell I'm going to do. Do I act normal and wait for the sword of Damocles to fall, or do I confess all? No! Oh God, what a mess. What a bloody, stinking mess I've made of things.'

Outside once more, Carmichael ventured an opinion. 'Looks like he's in a bit of a pickle, doesn't it, sir?'

'Looks like he's just given himself a first-class

189

motive for the second murder as well as the first, my lad,' and Falconer rubbed his hands together with glee. 'Odds-on favourite is our Mr Manningford, and we haven't had to do anything – he's trussing himself up like a turkey without any help from us.'

Chapter Eighteen

Thursday 16th July – afternoon

I

At the vicarage, the day had started badly for the Swainton-Smythes, and, as lunch drew to a close, it was not improving. Lillian, after being dispatched for a lie-down while Falconer and Carmichael questioned her husband, had awoken refreshed but emotional (or, rather more sober but spoiling for a fight, as a less kindly person might describe her state).

She had insisted on a pre-luncheon gin and tonic to steady her nerves and had, without consultation with Rev. Bertie, uncorked a bottle of Chardonnay to accompany their tinned salmon salad. When she had cleared away the plates and returned to the table with the cheese board in one hand and a decanter of port in the other, her husband sent up a silent prayer to St Jude, and prepared to batten down his emotional hatches. It looked like Lillian was on course for a real bender, and all he could do was to be there and protect her from herself.

II

On their way back to Market Darley, Falconer had made a quick diversion home and pressed his offending shirtsleeve, before they continued their journey back to headquarters. There, they spent a little over an hour at their desks, and then had lunch in the staff canteen (sausage, egg, chips, beans, tomatoes, mushrooms and fried bread for Carmichael: tuna salad and a baked potato for Falconer), before returning to Castle Farthing to resume their questioning.

III

They started at The Old School House. Martha Cadogan answered the door to them and, in doing so, let out her new canine companion, who capered round the policemen's ankles and leapt up at them in an ecstasy of welcome.

'Get down, Buster, and let the gentlemen come through the door. What will they think of us, keeping them on the doorstep like this?'

She walked ahead of them a small, white-haired figure with a slight hesitation in her slow step that belied her arthritis. 'Come into the kitchen. The kettle's hot and I've just baked some scones.'

'That's very kind of you, Miss Cadogan,' Falconer acknowledged.

'Don't mention it, young man. I suppose you've

come about young Lowry. Such an unpleasant young man, he was. Rosemary in the shop was giving a news broadcast when I called in for my paper. She says she doesn't gossip, but she's dreadful.'

Had no one a good word to say about the dead in this village? 'Would you mind telling me anything you can remember about the fallings-out at the party last night?' asked Falconer, helping himself to a warm, golden-topped scone. Carmichael already had four on his plate, split and filled with butter and jam, teacup beside his heaped plate. He was certainly a hard worker where food was concerned. His notebook was on the old pine kitchen table, the ribs of the table-top's grain raised with many years of scrubbing. The sergeant's pen (he had collected a new one from the office, when Falconer had forcibly regained possession of the one he had lent him earlier) was held at the ready in his right hand, while his left conveyed the unexpected culinary largesse to his mouth.

'I heard some disagreeable exchanges while I was sitting with Lillian and Bertie, but I turned a deaf ear at those points. I didn't want another run-in with that young man, after what he had done to poor Buster.'

'What about later? Just before Lowry left? I understand your nephew-in-law saw him home.'

'That's right. I'd gone to the bar to 'stand my round', as I think the saying goes. Bertie doesn't have a large stipend' (here Carmichael looked mildly alarmed at what he initially assumed to be a personal medical term) 'and Lillian has no opportunity for paid work with her parish duties.'

(And her drinking, thought Falconer.) 'It was while I was at the bar that what I think of as "the big scene" occurred. It was all very nasty and spiteful – and unnecessary – accusing the Brigadier of murder, calling the Rollasons bad parents, putting down his own wife, then letting the cat out of the bag about you-know-who. I didn't get involved. I might have got a kick myself for my pains, who knows? No, I just kept my distance, and then dear Bertie came over and took him away. It quite ruined the party, and we'd all been having such a nice time.'

'What did you do after the vicar took Lowry home?'

'Oh, I toddled back here.'

'On your own?'

'Of course, on my own! This is Castle Farthing, Inspector, not the East End. I only had to turn into Drovers Lane and I could cut down the access road to my own back gate. It's no distance at all, and I always carry a torch in my bag – so handy for extra light, and not a bad little weapon, should I ever have need of such a thing.'

Whew! 'What did you do when you got in?'

'I rang Bertie to see that all was well, then it was just my usual bedtime routine. I put out some food and water for the hedgehogs and any stray cats, fed Buster, made myself some hot milk and took myself off to bed.'

'Thank you very much, Miss Cadogan.'

'I'm not sorry he's dead, you know,' she continued, as if she had not heard him, 'bad blood will out. He'd probably have ended up just like his great-uncle, and when I think of all the unplea-

193

santness he caused during his lifetime, well, the village is better off without the pair of them. At least that poor wife and those children of his might benefit from their misfortune. If Michael inherited from Reg, and I doubt Michael made a will at his age, why, Kerry can stop worrying about where the next penny's coming from now. They never divorced, you know, so I suppose it'll all go to her.'

This last had never occurred to Falconer. He had just assumed that she was his ex-wife. He would have to check that one out as soon as he saw her again, as it put rather a different light on the matter of motive, in her case.

IV

During the afternoon, the heat had continued to build and it was searingly hot. It was certainly too hot to be sitting outside, and at The Old Manor House Brigadier Malpas-Graves led them into a blessedly cool sitting room at the north end of the house. French windows were opened wide to the garden, and a large-bladed electric fan hummed from the centre of the ceiling, sending deliciously cool draughts round the room.

Joyce Malpas-Graves was sitting at an embroidery frame, a pair of half-glasses perched on the end of her nose. 'Hello, Inspector; hello, Sergeant. You look all hot and bothered. Can I get you a cold drink?'

'Yes please.' Carmichael was feeling like a boiled lobster in his shirt and long trousers, and thought longingly of his baggy Bermuda shorts.

As if in an act of telepathy Joyce added, 'I should go back to your lovely bright beachwear tomorrow, Sergeant. So much less chafing in the heat, don't you think?' and, leaving him blushing at what this implied, she stabbed her embroidery needle viciously into her work and bustled from the room.

'Heart of gold, that old girl,' commented her husband, gazing after her fondly.

Motioning them towards a battered leather chesterfield sofa, the Brigadier took the seat opposite where his wife had been sitting and opened the conversation himself. 'Come about the Lowry boy, have you?'

'That's right, sir. Wondered if you could tell us about last night?'

'Certainly can. Ah, here's Joyce with the jolly old drinks. Take one, take one, don't be shy.' He drank deeply. 'That's better. Now, where was I? Last night? Yes. Got myself all steamed up again, I'm afraid.'

'Yes, you did, didn't you, Godfrey. For shame.' Joyce had resumed her needlework and spoke without looking up.

'I did, old girl. Ought to be ashamed of myself at my age, twice in as many weeks.'

'What did you get steamed up about, Brigadier?'

'That blasted young pup Lowry only accused me of murdering his great-uncle. Me – a murderer? Oh, I know now how ridiculous it sounds, but in that atmosphere – and I'd had a few pink gins...' he tailed off.

'How many, I wonder?' The voice sounded again from the embroidery frame.

195

'Far too many, m'dear. I'm going to have to keep a weather eye on just how many I sup. Gets the sap rising and I forget my age – and my dignity, I suppose. Blow me, I nearly popped old Reg one over my veg and stuff, and there I was again, ready to mix it with his great-nephew. Well, I'll be blowed! Hope I didn't put the evil eye on them – you hear about that sort of thing out east, but I never really thought there was anything in it. Joyce, you don't think...?'

'Don't be ridiculous, Godfrey.'

'Quite right. Silly of me.'

The little sitting room was a testament to an army family that had travelled widely. On an assortment of carved and inlaid tables were items of brassware, carvings, and contorted figures of wood and stone. A small display cabinet held delicately carved pieces of ivory and jade, and in the empty fireplace sat a fair-sized copper gong. The walls and mantelpiece displayed framed photographs of a rather younger Brigadier Malpas-Graves in uniform, and what were, from the family resemblance, his father and other male relatives, similarly uniformed and variously decorated with medals.

'Another drink, Inspector?'

'I'm sorry, Mrs Malpas-Graves, I was miles away, admiring the room. Very masculine,' Falconer replied, tactfully but insincerely.

'Used to be my father's study. Got very fond memories of running my train set round in here when I was a nipper.'

'Godfrey! You used to do that after we were married.'

The Brigadier cleared his throat loudly in embarrassment and turned back towards the policemen. 'Anything else I can help you with, gentlemen?'

'Can you tell me what you did after Lowry created that big scene and was led off the premises?'

'Old George went round with some more food, and his wife chivvied people along to have another drink, but the atmosphere had been spoilt. We didn't stay long after that. Just pottered on home.'

'What did you do when you got home?'

'I went straight to bed, inspector.' Joyce's voice sounded once more from behind her work.

'And I stayed up with a night-cap to cool off a bit, get my head showered. Sat in here and read my book for a bit.'

'What time did you go up to bed?'

'No idea, old boy. No clock in here. See?'

'Did you notice, Mrs Malpas-Graves?'

'Hardly, Inspector. We have separate rooms.'

And that appeared to be that, except for the fact that the Brigadier's left wrist wore a rather elderly, but nonetheless handsome, Rolex watch.

'No clock, my arse,' muttered Falconer as the door closed behind them.

V

The curtains at the downstairs window of Jasmine Cottage were closed, and the cottage looked empty, deserted, somehow forlorn, but their second summons was answered and the door pulled open for them to enter. Kerry Long was a sorry sight. Her hair was tangled, her face devoid of make-up, her nose and eyes were red and swollen from crying. When she spoke, her voice was thick with unshed tears, and Carmichael's soft heart went out to her.

'I'm sorry, I know I look a state. Come in so I can shut this door. I don't want to be an object of pity.'

She led them into the darkened front room and just flopped on to the settee, like a marionette that has had all its strings suddenly severed. 'You've come about Mike?'

'I'm afraid so.'

'I just can't believe he's dead,' and with this, her body was wracked with sobs.

Falconer stood like a statue, moved and irritated at the same time, by the only show of grief they had encountered in connection with either death. It was Carmichael who showed a more practical approach, and he immediately sat down beside her, put an arm round the young widow and handed her a crumpled handkerchief from his trouser pocket. Kerry took this gratefully and buried her face in his shoulder, still sobbing like a small child.

'Tea, sir.'

'Sorry, Carmichael?'

'Go and make some tea.'

'Tea?'

'Go to the kitchen and make some tea – good and strong, and very sweet. I think Ms Long could do with some.'

Stunned at this reversal of roles, Falconer walked like an automaton to the kitchen and put the kettle on. Maybe there was more to Carmichael than met the eye. The younger man had reacted instinctively with compassion to the young woman's pain, and Falconer realised with surprise that he was grateful not to be burdened with that himself.

When he returned with a tray holding three brimming mugs and the sugar bowl, it was to a much less emotionally charged scenario. Carmichael still sat beside Kerry, but she no longer clung to him. Her tears had ceased for now, and she had managed to find time to run a comb through her hair, an open handbag at her feet testament to this last.

'Have you got any biscuits?' Carmichael asked her.

'Yes. In the cupboard beside the cooker.'

'Well, you run along and wash your face while I get them. Then we can have our tea and see how you're feeling.'

She left the room with a watery smile and Carmichael disappeared down the hall to the kitchen. Falconer just stared. Well!

VI

'I know we weren't together any more, but we had two kids and we had history. You can't just switch off all those years together as if they hadn't happened. And it doesn't matter if you're not in love any more, all of the feelings don't go away.'

They had drunk their tea, and Carmichael had

199

sugared Kerry's brew as heavily as he had laced his own. He had over-dunked ginger nuts and managed to look genuinely surprised when they broke off and fell into his cup, fishing the soggy remnants out with a sausage-like finger. He had persuaded her to eat a couple of biscuits, and his light-hearted and practical approach had worked. Slowly she had relaxed a little and now, the mugs empty, the biscuit plate decorated with only a few crumbs, she was able to speak coherently.

'I know he treated me rotten at times, and I know he said some nasty stuff last night. I expect people might think I ought to be glad he's dead, but I'm not. I just wish he'd paid the mainten-ance regular and spent more time with the kids. That's all I wanted. And I'm not glad. He was my husband after all.'

'You never divorced?' Falconer needed to check, but his voice was subdued. He was walking on eggshells here and had no wish to provoke another storm of tears.

'No. Never got around to it. There wasn't really anyone else, so what was the point of more expense?' She broke off here and there was silence for a couple of minutes, neither of the men wish-ing to intrude on her thoughts.

'And there's the children,' she resumed in a smaller voice. 'I haven't had the heart to tell them yet. How can you tell your own kids that their daddy's dead?'

'There, there,' soothed Carmichael, putting an arm around her as she threatened to dissolve, once more, into tears. 'Where are the kiddies?'

His pragmatic words saved the situation, and she

pulled herself together. 'I could hardly send them to school, not with what's happened. Auntie's got them. They're playing shop with a load of old packets and boxes at the back of hers. She's given them her jar of foreign coins she's fished out of the till over the years, to use as money.'

'Good old Auntie,' said Carmichael quietly.

'Yeah. She's been great.'

There was one thing Falconer needed to know before he went any further, and this seemed as good a moment as any to intervene. 'Do you know if your husband made a will, Ms Long?'

Kerry wrinkled her forehead in thought. 'I'm sure it never crossed his mind. Wills are for old people,' she said naively. 'You can check through his stuff but I doubt you'll find anything. Why do you want to know?'

'Because if he made no will and you were never divorced, everything will come to you, including what his great-uncle left him.'

As they walked back to the car, Carmichael's face was a picture of barely suppressed confrontation, and Falconer heeded the unspoken warning. It did not, however, stop him from thinking.

VII

Back at headquarters, jackets over the backs of their chairs, ties off and an oscillating fan (which Falconer had collected on another quick diversion to his home) humming on the desk between them, they began to go over what they had so far.

'What is it with bedtimes last night?' asked Falconer, expecting no answer. 'One: Marian Warren-Browne takes a sleeping tablet and doesn't hear her husband come to bed.' He held up a finger. 'Two:' he held up another, 'Paula Covington goes out like a light, leaving George to clear up on his own. Three: Rebecca Rollason cries herself to sleep and Nick stays up to cool off – oh yeah? Four: Piers Manningford can say what he likes, as his wife is so conveniently away on business, and five:' here he indicated with a thumb, as he had run out of fingers, 'Mrs Brigadier doesn't even share a bedroom with her husband. Damn and blast it! I forgot to ask the vicar what time they turned in. There's something going on there some-where between that lot, and I intend to find out exactly what it is. I will not have the wool pulled over my eyes and be lied to.'

'You never asked Kerry Long what she did when she got home, sir.' This was the first men-tion Carmichael had made of her since they had left her cottage.

'Didn't need to, lad,' Falconer replied. Of course he hadn't needed to. She could have slipped out at any time while the children were asleep and no one would have been any the wiser, but he was not going to voice this opinion in Carmichael's pre-sence, at least not for now.

Changing the subject he said, 'That Marian Warren-Browne's always popping sleeping tab-lets. I'd dearly love to know which ones they are, but I don't think Dr Christmas would play ball just at the moment – at least not until we get official confirmation of their presence in Lowry's stomach, and he did say he never prescribed that

202

brand. Still, I suppose the ones he does prescribe might not have agreed with her. There's always an outside chance. Anyway, who do you think is still in the frame, Carmichael?'

'Piers Manningford for me, sir. By the way, we didn't go and see Mrs Romaine today.'

'So we didn't. But I've a feeling that, after last night's little revelation, she'll have a full-time job on her hands sweet-talking the birthday boy.'

'It could've been him, sir.'

'You're right. I hadn't even thought of that. We'd better catch up with those two. Anyone else?'

'That Rollason chap's got a nasty temper on him. Look how steamed up he was this morning. Reckon he'd kill to protect that wife and son of his. And what about that postmaster?'

'What about him?'

'Treats that old wife of his like a princess – her and her headaches. Fair wraps her in cotton wool and worships the ground she walks on. I bet he could turn real nasty, given the right circumstances.'

And there ended the gospel according to Acting DS Carmichael, comforter of young widows and sage before his time.

VIII

Early evening at the vicarage saw Lillian Swainton-Smythe very drunk and holding forth to her long-suffering husband. 'This parish is positively going to the dogs, Bertie. And just what are you going to do about it? What – are – you – going – to

– do – about – it?' she spaced her words in an effort not to slur them.

'What do you mean, going to the dogs, Lillian? Explain yourself.'

'You know ezackly what I mean. First there's that pig of an old man – that dirty old git – making trouble for everyone – everyone – including you. Look at Christmas. Look at Harvest. Thieving old git.'

'Lillian!'

'Well he was. Trouble with you, is you're too Christian. Well, I'm no' 'fraid to tell the truth. Then there was that pois'nous nephew.'

'Great-nephew,' corrected her husband.

'Lousy nephew. And don' nit-pick. I've forgo'n what I was sayin' now.' She paused to take a swig of almost neat gin. 'Oh yeah, that nephew – oh pawdon me, grea' nephew – of his, treatin' his own family like dirt. Kicked poor li'l Buster, he did. Poor li'l Buster! An' look at las' night. Pois'nous to everyone he was. An' who takes 'im home? Good li'l Christian vicar Bertie. Well, he's dead now. They both are and good ri'ance. P'raps there is a God after all. Here's to you, God.' She drank deeply again.

'Lillian! Behave yourself.'

'Behave myself? Wha' about telling those adult'rers t' behave themselves, then? There they are – both married to other people – and shaggin' the arse off each other ev'ry oppot ... opporuti ... opportun'ty they get.' Finally she got the word out.

'That's only hearsay.'

'Iss the truth. You could see it in their faces las'

night if you weren't too much of a saint. An' I say wha' are you goin' to do abou' it? Eh, Bertie? Eh?'

'Lillian, you're drunk.'

'Well, for your inf'mation, to paraphrase some-one or other – I forge' who, bu' it doesn't matter – tomorrow I shall be sober,' here she broke off to smother a hiccough, 'bu' you will still be a coward. Because tha's what you are, a moral coward. You won't face anyone with their sin – you jus' go on forgivin'.'

'Yes, and that's why I'm still here with you.' Rev. Bertie had been goaded beyond endurance.

'How dare you!'

'No, how dare you, Lillian. I'm going out for a walk now. I don't expect to find you up when I get back. I'll get my own supper.' And with that he walked out.

'The hell you will,' his wife called after him, refilling her glass (just gin this time), one eye closed so that she could focus enough to pour. 'Well, I'm goin' to do somethin' abou' it, even if you're too frightened to, you lily-livered ol' fart.' Pulling open her handbag, she began to paw through it until she found her address book.

Chapter Nineteen

Friday 17th July – morning and afternoon

I

Friday began in a somewhat more leisurely and more relaxed manner for Harry Falconer than had the preceding day. He arose at the alarm clock's summons, showered and, standing naked in his dressing area, opened a wardrobe door to reveal a row of crisp, impeccably-pressed shirts in a range of pastel colours. Selecting one in a delicate eau-de-nil cotton – short-sleeved, for it promised to be another sweltering day – he dressed and sauntered down to his gleaming kitchen to greet Mycroft.

There he brewed coffee, scrambled eggs and cut up a morsel of smoked salmon. The last two, laid on a slice of wholemeal toast for him, the latter placed in a stainless steel bowl for the cat, put both of them in an even better mood.

Pausing only to put the dishes in the dishwasher and make sure his Siamese familiar was adequately provided with dried food and fresh water, he checked his appearance in the hall mirror, adjusted a hair or two, and grabbed his car keys. He left the house whistling.

'Damn, damn, damn!' For the third time he turned the ignition key to hear only a melancholy 'clunk'. Pulling the bonnet release catch under the dashboard, he got out to see what he could see. Lots of lumps of metal, pipes, wires and dangly bits, and all too grubby to think about touching. Yep, that's what was always there. Shutting the bonnet and kicking petulantly at a tyre, he re-entered the house to telephone the garage. A further call secured him transport for the day and, his good mood completely evaporated, it was with a heavy heart that he heard a clarion call outside the house and opened the front door to Carmichael.

So horrified was he by the sight of the rust-pocked, once-white Skoda with its dull blue near-side wing, that he hardly gave his sergeant a glance. Perching as gingerly as he could on the 'fun' tiger-striped passenger seat cover, his feet surrounded by crisp packets and sweet papers, he stared miserably ahead of him, just wishing the journey over with.

'Car playing up, then?' Carmichael, at least, was chirpy.

'Yes.'

'Know what's wrong with it?'

'No.'

'Garage going to fix it today?'

'Yes.'

'So you'll be all right for tomorrow, then?'

'Yes.'

'You know them sleeping tablets that Mrs Warren-Browne takes?'

'Yes.' Falconer was going for gold in the terseness event.

'I found out what they are.'

'You what?' That woke him up.

'I said I found out which ones she takes.'

'How? Old Christmas was really tight-arsed about divulging individual patients' details.'

'I asked her.'

'Who?' asked Falconer un-grammatically.

'That Mrs Warren-Browne. I rang and asked her. Said we needed to know for purposes of elimination. Said would she tell me, so I could confirm it with Dr Christmas. That way I reckoned she wouldn't lie to me.'

'Good man. Well thought out. And what are they?' A flame of hope sprang up in Falconer's breast.

'Zopiclone.' And was immediately extinguished. Oh well, it had been an outside chance anyway, and it was at least one more detail out of the way.

At the office a copy of the post-mortem report awaited them, confirming the presence of a large dose of diazepam in the stomach and bloodstream of Michael Lowry, late of the village of Castle Farthing. The report also confirmed that the second death had been a carbon copy of the first, and had probably occurred between the hours of 10 pm and 3 am. This could be narrowed, at the earlier end, by the time that Lowry had left the pub and – if he were telling the truth – the evidence of the vicar.

A short report from forensics confirmed that the wire used in the second murder was from the same roll as that used in the first, cut ends from each piece having been matched, so at least they were only looking for one murderer, rather than a first murderer (as Shakespeare would probably have put it) and a copycat murderer.

208

Paperwork kept them from Castle Farthing for the remains of the morning, and their visit to the Romaines was postponed for the time being. The only interruption they received during the first half of that day was a telephone call to Falconer, to inform him that his car needed a new starter motor, that it would cost a ridiculous amount of money when labour and VAT were added, and that his vehicle would be delivered back to his house later that day and the keys put through his letterbox and, finally, would he like to give his credit card details for ease of payment? As he replaced the receiver, Falconer turned to Carmichael and said, only half-jokingly, 'Sergeant, I wish to report a mugging.'

II

They were just finishing their lunch in the canteen when the duty desk sergeant approached their table. 'I've just had a call from Carsfold, sir,' he informed Falconer. 'There's been a report of a noisy domestic in Castle Farthing. They've sent an officer to deal with it, but the duty officer from Carsfold had the nous to check with us. It's a couple you've spoken to with regard to the murders, so I thought you might like to know about it.'

'Fire away, Bob.'

'Couple called Manningford. Address, Pilgrims' Rest, Sheepwash Lane. Of any interest?'

Falconer dabbed at his mouth with a paper napkin. 'Thanks a lot. We're on our way. Come along Carmichael, surely you can eat faster than that?'

Carmichael could, and was only a few steps behind the inspector as he strode out of the building, then slowed abruptly as he remembered just what carriage awaited him. They'd have to go by pumpkin until his carriage was back on the road.

III

There was no sign of a disturbance when they reached Pilgrims' Rest, no sound at all coming from the property. Whoever had come out from Carsfold had obviously calmed things down for the time being, though for how long, Falconer did not wish to speculate, given the probable subject matter of the disagreement.

A ring on the doorbell brought Piers Manningford in answer, sporting a magnificent, and obviously recent, black eye. Dorothy, skulking in the sitting room, had a split and swollen lower lip and red-rimmed eyes.

'I suppose even you lot knew about this before I did,' she accused the two policemen, her whole body trembling with rage. 'Him and that trollop next door. How could you?' she turned on her husband, eyes blazing.

'I'm going to make some coffee,' he said, and scuttled from the room, tail metaphorically between his legs.

'That's right, run away. Run away like you always do, you snivelling little worm.'

'Mrs Manningford, if you could calm down a little, we'd like a word with you. We can speak to your husband later.'

'You speak to him. I never want to speak to or see him again.' She stopped and took a shuddering breath. 'I'm sorry. None of this is your fault. I do apologise. How can I help you?'

'Perhaps you'd like to tell us why it was necessary for an officer to call here earlier?'

'Of course.' She sat down, leaning forward in her chair, knees together, her hands clasped tightly in her lap, fighting for control. 'I've been away for a few days on business, as you probably already know. I got back yesterday afternoon and, apart from Piers being a bit jumpy, everything seemed fine. Then about six-thirty my mobile rang. Of course, I assumed it was business and took it to my study to take the call, but it was Lillian – the vicar's wife – and she was absolutely stinking drunk. At first, I tried to get her off the line, thought she was raving when she said she hadn't wanted to ring the house phone in case Piers answered and tried to stop her speaking to me.

'Then she started talking about Piers and that whore next door, saying they'd been having an affair. That got my attention, I can tell you. Artist, my foot! More of a painted lady.'

'Did you believe her?'

'Yes I did. A lot of things suddenly clicked into place. Then she said that I should have been at Clive's birthday "do", as it had been broadcast to the whole village and everyone was talking about it.'

'It must have been very difficult for you.' Falconer tried to sound as supportive as possible in the hope that she would remain calm and continue with her narrative.

'It was, but I wasn't going to go off the deep end just then. Oh, I got rid of Lillian. She sounded almost on the point of passing out anyway. I knew I had a very important meeting to attend this morning, so I decided to stay calm, get on with things, then face him with it today.

'I felt quite devious, telling him it was an all-day meeting and not to expect me till six, then turning up here at midday to surprise him. And, oh boy, did I surprise him.' Her eyes filled with tears and her tale ground to a halt.

'It's all right, Mrs Manningford. Carry on when you feel ready.'

'I'm fine,' she sniffed, jabbed at her eyes with a tissue, blew her nose and continued. 'The house was completely empty when I got back. I'd let myself in very quietly, crept upstairs to see if they were up there, but there was no one in.'

'What did you do then?'

'I went next door. I rang the bell, but nobody answered, looked through the front windows but couldn't see anyone, so I decided to go round the back. Couldn't see anyone there either, but I could hear voices – oh, and noises. Do you know, I caught them at it – actually at it, like a couple of dogs – in that seedy little shed of hers at the end of the garden? God, it makes me feel sick just to think about it.'

At that point, Piers re-entered the room carrying a tray. 'You filthy bastard!' Dorothy screamed, and, leaping to her feet, she pushed past him, sending the tray and its contents flying. 'I'm going to pack a bag this very minute. I'll be gone a couple of days, and when I get back I don't want to find you here, do you understand?' she shrieked from the doorway, then stamped off up the stairs leaving her husband covered in hot coffee grounds and embarrassment.

They left him to it. There seemed little he could contribute at that point, and they could always return when things were a little calmer and Piers had only a stained reputation to contend with.

IV

Next door at The Beehive, Cassandra Romaine admitted them with a rueful smile, and conducted them through to the kitchen. Their first good look at her confirmed that she had not escaped the fall-out of her adulterous actions scot-free. One cheek was bruised and there were scratch-marks on her forehead.

Seeing the direction of their glances she said, 'Don't go thinking this is Clive's handiwork. You've not got a second domestic on your hands. This,' she pointed to her injuries, 'is courtesy of Madam Dorothy. She did this to me before blacking Piers's eye.'

'And who split her lip?' Falconer was curious.

'She did that herself. Swung so hard at Piers that she lost her balance and fell on to my easel. Bled over a perfectly good water colour, the cow.' This, somehow, was not surprising. Piers did not look as if he had the guts to stand up to his domineering wife.

'Is that all you called about?'

'No, actually,' said Falconer. 'We needed to

213

check on your movements – both of you – after you returned from The Fisherman's Flies on Wednesday evening.'

'Oh, that's an easy one. We had our own cosy little domestic, all private and almost civilised. Of course, Clive was fuming when we got in. Got all self-righteous with me and said he'd been made a right fool of in front of everyone, and what did I think I was doing, playing the tart on my own doorstep?'

'Very unpleasant.'

'It was. But I took a shot in the dark, and luckily hit the bulls-eye. I asked him about that new PA who'd just started in his office, and who just seemed to keep cropping up in conversation recently. Well, that shut him up. I've had my suspicions for a week or two, and this more or less confirmed it. He started getting all conciliatory – you know, I can forgive this once, but you'll have to be a better wife to me blah, blah, blah. Well, he's still sulking. He's in the study if you want his version of things. He got home about half an hour ago – said he had a headache and would work from home this afternoon.'

'Thank you, Mrs Romaine. Just one more thing before we have a word with him. What time did you both go to bed on Wednesday night?'

'About two o'clock,' she replied. 'And to separate bedrooms, I might add.'

And she had still been acting like a bitch on heat that very lunchtime, thought Falconer. He almost admired her dedication.

'Thank you. We'll just go through and have that word with your husband before we leave.'

214

Clive Romaine had little to add to the sorry tale, merely giving it a different spin to put himself in a better light, and within ten minutes they were walking back to Carmichael's Skoda.

'I'm sorry about my appearance today, sir,' said Carmichael apologetically.

'What's wrong with it?' For the first time that day Falconer took a good look at his sergeant – black trousers, short-sleeved white shirt, pale blue tie – whatever was the man talking about? For once he looked very respectable.

'Well, having to wear this old stuff. All my best clobber's in the wash.' (Glory be! thought Falconer, and long may it remain there.) 'But don't worry. I'll get it all pressed nice tonight – I won't let you down two days in a row.'

V

Just a couple of miles to the south of Castle Farthing, a car was travelling away from the village on the Carsfold Road which was, for this time of day, unusually devoid of other traffic. On leaving the village, the car had accelerated to a little over eighty miles an hour and held that speed. The face of its sole occupant was set in a grim mask compounded of determination and despair. The eyes that raked the road ahead were lit with grim purpose.

As the vehicle approached a long, tight bend to the left there was no slackening of its speed, nor was there when it reached the bend and started to slide out of control. As it slewed wildly, the driver pulled once and futilely on the steering wheel, too late to correct the angle of progress, right foot pumping convulsively on the brake pedal. Yet still there was no decrease in its speed and it left the road, crossed a narrow band of rough grass and wild flowers, and ploughed headlong into the trunk of a venerable horse chestnut tree.

The impact crushed the front end of the vehicle and shattered the windscreen, throwing around the upper half of the driver like a rag doll.

In the silence that followed the squeal of tyres, the crunch of twisting and tearing metal and the tinkle of breaking glass, there came no movement from within the vehicle. The driver hung, slumped sideways in the seatbelt, and unmoving. All was still.

Chapter Twenty

Friday 17th July – late afternoon

I

It was almost six-thirty and Falconer was thinking about going home, about dinner and a little piano practice, when his telephone rang. Damn! It had better be something trivial. He answered it and, as he listened, his face became progressively more glum. With an ill-tempered, 'Damn, blast, bugger and bum!' he replaced the receiver.

Carmichael looked across at him in surprise.

'What's up, sir? Is it your car?'

'If only it were. Nothing so simple. There's been an RTA on the Carsfold Road.'

'But that's Traffic, isn't it?'

'It was when it happened. Now it's ours. Dorothy Manningford was the driver.'

'She's not dead, is she?' Falconer could see a body count going on in Carmichael's eyes.

'No, but she's injured and unconscious.'

'What happened?'

'It would seem that she lost control of the car on a fairly tight left-hand bend, went off the road and hit a tree. No witnesses. Someone driving by saw the car and dialled 999 on their mobile, so we're not even sure exactly when it happened.'

'She was on her own?'

'Yes, but it took some time to cut her free, apparently. She's in the ITU in Market Darley County Hospital. Come on, we'd better get ourselves over there, see what we can find out.'

II

The ITU sister went through Dorothy's injuries with them before allowing them to look in on her. 'She's still unconscious, although there's no skull fracture. Broken right femur, left ankle and right tibia, several broken ribs, severe bruising, and some cuts and abrasions. She's lucky to be alive.'

'But she will live?'

'The prospects are good. We've not detected any signs of internal injury or brain swelling, which is

217

good. It'll be a long road to recovery though, and there's no telling when she'll wake up.'

'Do you think she'll remember what happened?'

'Who knows? It's doubtful, though. So often the accident itself, and sometimes quite a few hours before it, are wiped from the memory banks. It might come back in time, it might not.'

'Can we take a look?'

'Just for a minute. She's already got someone sitting with her.'

As Falconer and Carmichael entered the hospital room they saw Dorothy, head swathed in bandages, face cut and bruised, one arm in plaster, one leg plastered and raised in traction. A cage under the sheet was an obvious protection for her (probably plastered) broken ankle. A couple of plastic bags suspended above the bed snaked feed lines towards the back of her left hand. There were monitor wires attached to her chest just below her neckline and a ventilator hissed as it fed her lungs with air. A heart monitor by the bedside beeped the news that she was still in there, fighting.

They also saw, his back to them, the inevitable black-cassocked figure sitting by the bed, head bent in prayer. 'Rev. Swainton-Smythe, what a surprise. Third time lucky, eh? Except this one's still alive.'

The vicar turned to look at them. 'Inspector, Sergeant, I had to come. Not only is Dorothy one of my parishioners – one of my flock, if you like – but I also happen to think that this dreadful accident is all Lillian's and my fault.'

'Is that a confession, or are you just exercising your guilt muscle?' Falconer was flushed with anger. Would no one rid him of this accursed cleric?

'Don't be flippant, Inspector. Just give me a chance to explain and I'll go. I can pray just as well somewhere else. I've got a quick one to send up to St Anthony for Aunt Martha, and I think I might also say one for Lillian as well,' he finished, matching Falconer, 'flip' for 'flip'.

'Go on.'

'You saw how Lillian was yesterday morning. I can't believe you didn't notice she was...'

'A little tired and emotional?'

'Thank you for your tact. Yes, and she got more tired and emotional as the day wore on, to the point where she was, shall we say, roaring tired and intensely emotional.' Falconer could imagine it, and involuntarily shuddered. 'Exactly! And when she's like that, she does rather get a bee in her bonnet. This time she thought the whole parish was going to the dogs. Then she got fixated with... Do you think we could continue this conversation out in the corridor? I know Dorothy's unconscious, but it is possible that she can hear all this.'

'Of course.'

Outside the room, the door firmly shut, Rev. Bertie continued his sorry tale. 'Lillian got all worked up about adultery. I'm usually very patient with her, but with all that's happened recently in the village I was feeling a little on edge myself. I'd just about had enough. I'd put up with it all day, hoping she'd just go to sleep, or pass out, or something, but she didn't. On and on she went, practically raving, and I just reached the end of my

219

tether. I walked out and left her to it.'

Why doesn't the man get on with it? Falconer thought. He's treating this like an embroidery competition. 'So what happened?'

'I didn't know anything had. I went for a long walk to clear my head, dropped in at the church for some quiet contemplation, and when I got in she was out cold on the bed, fully dressed and snoring like a drain. I slept in the spare room and didn't bother to wake her this morning. I knew she'd be feeling like death, and I just left her to it and went about my business – had an MU meeting as it happens.

'Then, when we were finishing a rather late lunch (not that she was able to eat much) she apologised for her behaviour and told me she'd done a very stupid thing.'

'Which was?' Falconer already knew the answer to this one, but he did not want to break the narrative thread.

'She'd phoned Dorothy on her mobile and told her all the gossip there had been about Piers and Cassandra Romaine. Well, as soon as I could, I cycled up to Pilgrims' Rest to see if there was anything I could do, but only Piers was there, looking somewhat the worse for wear. He said she'd packed a bag and stormed out just after you two left, and he had no idea where she'd gone. I made him some tea and sat with him for a while, then the phone rang with news of this terrible accident.'

'How did he take it?'

'Not very well. I brought him straight here and we waited for her to come out of theatre, but there was nothing he could do, so I took him home, got

Aunt Martha to sit with him, and came back to, er, put in a bit of overtime, I suppose you could call it. Do you want me to turn out my pockets now?'

'Don't bother. I'm hardly going to arrest you for misappropriation of a bedpan or illegal possession of grapes, am I?'

'I'll be off then. Goodbye.'

As he walked away from them Falconer said, 'Right, Carmichael, I want you to sit in with her in case she comes round. I'll make arrangements for you to be relieved later. This might have been an accident, pure and simple, and it might not. I want you to keep a watchful eye on her, and let me know if there's any news.'

'How will you get home, sir? We came in my car, remember?'

'I'll walk. It's not far, and the exercise will do me good.' And he would not have to have another ride in Carmichael's Skoda-badged motorised dustbin.

III

Back home, and after a light but healthy (naturally) supper, and half an hour of tinkling the ivories – with the odd bruise here and there – Falconer was sitting in his study, his mind turning over and over the Swainton-Smythes' connection with what he was beginning to think of as 'The Castle Farthing Curse'. Oh, how he wished for a nice, simple, town murder.

His first thoughts were of the vicar, whose presence at the scenes of death and injury was

221

getting a bit too ubiquitous for his liking. When he and Carmichael had first arrived in the village to call at Crabapple Cottage, there was Rev. Swainton-Smythe, left alone with both body and evidence, to do as he pleased. When they had returned to visit Mike Lowry's bed-sit, there he was again, all alone and unsupervised. When they had arrived at the County Hospital, guess who was at the patient's bedside? Got it in one – Reverend Swainton-Smythe, and not a nurse or a doctor in sight.

But could the reverend gentleman really have been responsible for one or all of the incidents? Falconer wracked his brain, trying to put together a case against him. Why Reg Morley? Mrs Swainton-Smythe (or Lillian the Lush, as he was now beginning to think of her) freely admitted that the old man had caused a lot of trouble in the parish (didn't everyone?), had been a thorn in her husband's side on many an occasion, from petty theft, through general troublemaking, to downright vandalism, although not all proven. Given the level of irritation and bad feeling that the old man caused, would this be enough to push a shepherd to cull one of his flock for the benefit of the rest? Could his wife's 'little failing' have helped to unbalance him mentally?

And what about Lowry? Had Swainton-Smythe seen a similar behaviour pattern developing there and put him down the way one does a rogue dog for sheep-worrying? Really, all this rustic nonsense was affecting his brain. There were far too many animals creeping into his reasoning. He would be turning into David Attenborough if he were not careful.

At that moment the telephone rang, disrupting his thoughts and bringing him back to the here and now. With a sigh of annoyance he lifted the receiver. 'Bob Bryant here, sir,' (was the man never off duty, or did he have a clone?). 'Just got the report in, on the car from that RTA on the Carsfold Road. Thought you ought to know what they found, right away.'

'Go on.'

'Brake pipes cut through, brake fluid must've bled away. She went off on that sharp left-hander. Must've tried to brake, nothing happened, and she lost control. Sorry to disturb you on your evening off, but I thought you'd be interested.'

'Thanks very much, Bob. That's along the lines of what I was expecting.'

Replacing the receiver, Falconer returned to his speculations. What possible motive could the vicar have for wanting rid of Dorothy Manningford? Think about it, he urged his brain, there must be something there. Yes, he had got it – Lillian's drunken telephone call. If Lillian had known her husband was guilty of the murders, she may have let something slip over the phone, in vino veritas. Then, she confesses to her husband what she has done, and off he races to see if Dorothy has dropped him in it. And she hasn't, so he 'fixes' her car.

And the same went for Lillian Swainton-Smythe. She may have 'removed' the first two victims because they were causing her husband anguish, upsetting people and generally disrupting the parish. Swainton-Smythe had said she had got a bee in her bonnet about adultery. Maybe she had thought that Piers would drive the car, or maybe she had said something in her inebriated ravings to Dorothy, to indicate her own guilt.

Here he ground to a halt, a large hole suddenly appearing in his neatly knitted garment of culpability. Lillian had told her husband what had happened, in the afternoon. When the vicar got to Pilgrims' Rest, Dorothy had already left, and he had said himself that he had attended a meeting that morning. Falconer hardly expected a bunch of mothers to lie for their pastor. And Lillian had been sleeping off a spectacular binge, followed by what sounded like a similarly spectacular hangover. She would have been incapable of walking the previous evening and, even if she had had the gall to stagger up to Pilgrims' Rest that morning bent on mischief, surely someone would have noticed her, the state she must have been in? No, the Swainton-Smythes looked well and truly out of it. He would have to start looking somewhere else for his murderer.

Piers Manningford was the most obvious choice, because his motives were the most simple. Falconer began to re-do the jigsaw puzzle, hoping he did not have too many pieces of drainpipe in the postman's leg. That accident, had it been an accident, would have been just a little bit too convenient, given that Dorothy Manningford was the moneyed one and held the purse-strings.

From the top then, Piers knew that Reg Morley knew that he and Cassandra Romaine had embarked on an adulterous relationship. (It sounded like a rather muddled thought, but Falconer knew what he meant.) Manningford knew he could not withstand blackmail, as Dorothy would want an explanation of where the money was going, so the only solution was to remove the old man. That way there would be no blackmail, and no opportunity for Morley to make the affair public knowledge. Strike one!

Lowry had made it pretty obvious, and publicly so, that he knew about it too. By now Manningford must have been almost insane with worry. Killing Lowry may have been the act of a desperate man, to remove the only other person who seemed to have direct knowledge of the illicit relationship. Maybe he thought that with Lowry gone and Morley not having had the chance to say a word, he could convince Dorothy that it was just malicious village gossip. If it were so, then it was a drowning man clutching at straws, but it was just plausible, given Manningford's probable state of mind after that outburst in The Fisherman's Flies. Strike two!

Then, just when he thinks he has got himself into a position he can talk his way out of, Lillian puts a spanner in the works and delivers a drunken sermon on adultery and the sins of the flesh to his wife. What was even more surprising was the cunning used by the old soak in ringing Dorothy's mobile, thus avoiding being fobbed off by Piers on the landline. So, Piers still thinks he's safe, as Dorothy lies doggo and bides her time, even setting him up with a little time trap of her own. Does the stupid man fall straight into it? Of course he does, led by vanity. And his dick.

Then the balloon goes up and Piers is caught

with his trousers down (and a pretty good left hook, if Falconer was not mistaken). All hell breaks loose: the man is scared witless he'll lose everything. What on earth is he going to do now? Do away with Lillian? That would solve nothing. No, he must get rid of Dorothy.

She was obviously going to walk out on him. Even if she threw him out first, she had her own car. She would drive it sooner or later. Cutting the brake pipes was money in the bank for him, literally. It was also crazy, but Manningford was probably not feeling particularly rational with all that had happened recently.

There he was, nice home, nice lifestyle, plenty of money, hot little bit on the side. All was well with his world. Then it just blew up in his face. How could he possibly have acted rationally as things went from bad to worse? Strike three! Except that Dorothy was still alive. That had not been part of the plan.

Falconer felt that he had really got under the man's skin and seen things from his perspective. All the other village grievances with Morley and Lowry had blinded him, distracted him from the obvious. What a fool he must have seemed to Manningford, running from one suspect to another like a sniffer dog with a cold. Well, he had got him now. He would apply for a warrant in the morning.

There were other things that he had to do, though, and do right away. Manningford knew that it was Lillian who had blown the whistle on him, but there was someone else who had direct knowledge of the affair and, although she had been discreet about it, Manningford knew that that person was Martha Cadogan. Falconer was not sure just how unbalanced the man was, but he was not about to take any chances with either of these women.

Picking up the phone, he dialled first The Old School House, hoping that the old lady had not already gone to bed. 'Miss Cadogan, it's Inspector Falconer here. I hope I haven't woken you.'

'Not at all, Inspector. I was watching the hedgehogs come for their supper. So sweet. I often sit up to watch them.'

'You're not outside, are you?'

'No. Why?'

'I haven't time to explain now, but I want you to do something for me. Don't ask any questions, just do it, and I'll call round to see you tomorrow and explain.'

'What is it you want me to do, Inspector?'

'Lock your doors, close and lock your windows, and don't answer the door to anyone. And if anyone should come to the door or try to get in, phone me immediately.' Here he gave her his home number.

'It seems most irregular, but you said you'd explain tomorrow?'

'Yes. Thank you for your co-operation, Miss Cadogan.'

Having repeated these instructions in a call to the vicarage, Falconer felt he had done all that he could for the day, and spent a restless night expecting the shrill summons of the telephone to rouse him at any moment.

Chapter Twenty-one

Saturday 18th July – morning and afternoon

I

Falconer had obtained his warrant and roused a still-sleeping Carmichael, who had only been relieved from his hospital bedside duties at 2 am. An official car and uniformed driver collected them, and they were at the door of Pilgrims' Rest by seven-thirty. Manningford was not yet up, and it took a while for him to answer the door. He was unshaven, his hair standing on end, his body wrapped in a blue-and-red-striped towelling robe. His eye was still bruised and swollen and he wore insomnia like an aura.

'Not at your wife's bedside, Mr Manningford?' Falconer was not feeling all sweetness and light, having slept little himself.

'With the police by her bedside I hardly felt welcome. I phoned to see if she'd come round.'

'Very thoughtful of you, I'm sure. Well, I'm afraid I'm not here to improve your day,' said Falconer, following him into the house. And with that the inspector produced the warrant and went through the formalities of arrest.

Piers seemed genuinely shocked, and sank into a chair as if his legs would no longer support him. His eyes were wide, his mouth hanging open in disbelief. 'Are you mad?'

'Not us, Mr Manningford.'

'Well what the hell is all this, then? Surely I'm the injured party. How on earth can you cast me as the villain of the piece because of a bit of extra-curricular rumpy-pumpy?'

'That's not what you've been charged with.'

'Then tell me how the hell things have come to this?'

'You knew your liaison with Mrs Romaine had been discovered by Mr Morley.'

'Yes, I admit that.'

'You do?'

'Yes. Cassie had been pretty sure it was him in the woods that day. Later on she was walking past the village green, and he saw her and recognised her even, though the light was going – she wears some pretty bright colours. And the look he gave her, she said, was so smug. Oh, he knew all right. Even had the arrogance to lift his hand and wave to her.'

'That's a very brave admission, considering you have no alibi for Morley's murder.'

'I was here all evening. I told you that. And Dorothy was here too.'

'Upstairs, if I remember correctly, engrossed in her work. Maybe she didn't hear you go out, or maybe she was covering for you, as she had no idea then what you'd been up to. It'll be very interesting to speak to your wife when she regains consciousness.'

'If she sticks to the truth, she'll tell you no different to what I've told you.'

'And then there was Lowry's murder, so soon

after his outburst about you and Mrs Romaine. How convenient for you that your wife was away and there's no one to account for your movements. No alibi, Mr Manningford.

'And neither have half the men in Castle Farthing, if you only but knew it.'

Falconer knew there had been something fishy going on during the final hour of Wednesday evening. There had been so much prevarication and evasion about what time various inhabitants of the village had retired to bed that he had begun to suspect a meeting of the local witches' coven.

'Explain yourself, Manningford.'

'There was a meeting, wasn't there.'

'I don't know, man. That's why I'm asking you. What meeting? Where? Who was there?'

'At The Old Manor House. It was the Brigadier's idea.'

'When?'

'Midnight.'

'What was it about? What was the purpose of this meeting?' Falconer asked. It might prove to be a coven yet.

'To try to put Mike Lowry out of business and run him out of town – village, whatever. We were going to try to get rid of him. Oh God, I don't mean kill him, just to get him to move on and leave us in peace.'

'Apart from you and the Brigadier, who else attended this little gathering?'

'All the others who had had a spot of trouble with him: George Covington, Alan Warren-Browne and Nick Rollason.'

And now Lowry was dead, thought Falconer.

That explained an awful lot of shifty looks. And where did that leave him? With just enough rope, he thought. Manningford, knowing he would have an alibi from at least four other people at midnight, could easily have slipped along to the garage first, then just turned up at The Old Manor House as if nothing had happened. For that matter, he could have gone along after the meeting just as easily. After all, Dorothy had been away and could not say whether he had been in or out, or what time he had left or returned.

As they drove Manningford over to Market Darley Falconer, however, still had a tiny morsel of uneasiness nagging at him. Manningford being the guilty party seemed to tie up all the loose ends, but had he, Falconer, missed something? Was there something he had been missing all along, and was it still dangling there, still loose and unnoticed?

II

Using his own car (heaven be praised!) this time, and accompanied only by Carmichael – who appeared to have been too tired to select anything controversial from his wardrobe that morning – they returned to Castle Farthing in the early afternoon to make the promised calls on Martha Cadogan and Lillian Swainton-Smythe.

They found Martha in her back garden securing a piece of trellis to the top of a low stretch of fencing. 'Hello you two,' she greeted them. 'Pass me those pliers will you? Buster got it into his head that the honeysuckle was blowing raspberries at

231

him and managed to pull this down in a revenge attack – little tinker. There now, one more twist. Done! Come inside while I put the kettle on.'

Once she had settled them at the kitchen table she listened, head to one side, as Falconer explained the reasoning behind his brief telephone call the night before, and the arrest that had occurred that morning. As his narrative ended, he expected to be deluged with a barrage of questions, the answers to which would fuel the boilers of the village gossip machine for many a day. Instead, however, she seemed not even to have been listening.

'Look at Buster out there now, chasing butterflies. Isn't he a darling? He's such a happy doggy here with me, and we do enjoy each other's company so much. I only wish I'd had him when he was a puppy. Oh, and I must tell you, one of the feral cats – you know, the ones I put food out for – actually let me stroke the top of its head this morning. It's been coming closer and closer for weeks now but I haven't taken any liberties. I've just waited. And today it let me touch it, and do you know, it actually purred. It was only for a few seconds, but it was like a little miracle. It's so wonderful, the power animals have to learn to trust. And such a sweet little robin has been coming to the bird-table every day for almost a fortnight, and then, just this morning when I'd put out the scraps, I actually saw a pair of goldfinches feeding. What a heart-lifting sight that was. Such beautiful little birds.'

'Fascinating, Miss Cadogan. You do seem to be blessed with the company of wildlife.'

'Indeed I am, young man; very blessed indeed.'

The woman is obsessed, thought Falconer as they left, absolutely besotted with animals and birds. She had not even asked how Dorothy Manningford was, seeming more concerned with her blessed feral cat.

III

A visit to the vicarage found another woman with but a single subject on her mind. They were admitted by a very quiet (and stone-cold sober) Lillian Swainton-Smythe, her face the picture of contrition.

She ushered them into the cheerless sitting room and sat in silence, while Falconer repeated what he had just told Martha Cadogan. Only when he had finished did she speak.

'It's all so terrible. It's like we've been cursed ever since that old man was killed. Bertie just cannot forgive himself for leaving Michael's bedsit unlocked that night. Over and over it he goes. If only he'd sat with him until he'd woken. If only he'd brought him back here for the night. If only there'd been a letterbox he could have slipped the key through. It doesn't matter how many times I tell him that he can't change what has already happened, he won't let it go. He says it's his fault that someone got in and murdered the young man, and it must be a judgement on his failure as a minister of God.

'He won't listen to a word I say, and I just don't know what to do with him. He's spent so much

233

time in that church praying for forgiveness and guidance that he can hardly get up out of a chair where his knees are so sore.

'And look at me. I'm no better. What do I do when my own husband is wracked with guilt and needs my support? I get absolutely blind drunk and cause another barrel-load of trouble by blowing the whistle on Piers Manningford, where, if I'd left well alone, he'd probably have talked his way out of it and stopped seeing Cassandra. But no, I have to put my size twelves in, don't I?'

'Please, Mrs Swainton-Smythe, this isn't doing you any good.'

'But it's the truth. I get on my moral soapbox, all fuelled up with gin, and Dorothy ends up at death's door with her marriage in tatters. It's all my fault.'

'If it's anyone's fault it's Mr Manningford's. He was the one conducting the affair, not you.'

'I had no right to interfere,' she said contritely.

'Mrs Manningford would have found out anyway. Lowry made sure of that by broadcasting the news on Wednesday night.'

'But I was the catalyst. I was the one that brought it to a sudden head – like a boil, if you like. And now Dorothy's lying in hospital in a coma, her body all bruised and broken. Oh, I do hope she comes round soon, just so I can apologise and beg her forgiveness.'

Good grief, thought Falconer. At their last visit, old Miss Cadogan hadn't one word to say on the recent village tragedies, but this woman was running on like – well, like a thing that ran on and on. His mind was too punch-drunk from Lillian's tirade to come up with a suitable description.

'There is one thing I'd like to confirm with you,' he interrupted, hoping to distract her, but at that moment they heard the sound of a key in the front door, and Rev. Bertie came through to join them, his face a picture of misery.

'Glad you've joined us, sir. Just something I need to check: a loose end I need to tie up. When you got back from seeing Lowry home,' (the vicar winced at the memory of what he considered his dereliction of duty) 'what time did you go to bed?'

'About eleven-thirty. Lillian'll tell you.'

'That's right. I stayed down for a little night-cap.'

I bet you did, thought Falconer, but managed to keep the thought out of his expression. 'What time did you go up, Mrs Swainton-Smythe?'

'I'm very much afraid I can't remember. I fell asleep in the chair. I don't remember a thing from Bertie going to bed until I woke up with an awful thirst, still in the chair, about half-past five.'

IV

On their way back to headquarters, what had seemed so certain to Falconer the previous evening and early this morning was turning to doubt. What if his reasoning had been flawed? What if he had arrested the wrong man? Manningford had seemed genuinely dumbfounded at his arrest. Could anyone be that good an actor?

And wasn't Lillian Swainton-Smythe behaving

rather like Lady Macbeth, in that she seemed so consumed with guilt? The Reverend Bertie may not have been present at that silly Boys' Own meeting at The Old Manor House, but what had his wife been up to? Was she dead drunk, or was she out and about with murderous intent – maybe even with no recollection whatsoever of her actions. God, that would be a real shit-kicker. How the hell would he prove that? Hell, he needed a holiday – or a lucky break.

Chapter Twenty-two

Monday 20th July – morning

I

It was a quarter past seven on Monday morning. Harry Falconer had just showered and dressed, and was about to sit down to his breakfast, when the phone rang. With a stern warning to Mycroft to keep well away from his master's kipper, he rose and walked over to the wall phone, listened for a minute or so, and replaced the receiver with a muttered 'thank you'.

So, Dorothy Manningford was awake, he thought, lightly buttering a slice of wholemeal bread. That should make for some very interesting questioning a little later. Even if she were unable to recall the 'accident' itself, she might have some light to shed on her husband's whereabouts on the night Reg Morley was murdered. If she had been covering up for him before, in the light of what had since happened, the gloves should be off now. If she had anything to tell, he had no doubt she would be more than willing to pour it out to him. Today could prove to be a very good day. Maybe this was the lucky break he had been hoping for.

A quick phone call secured an arrangement to pick Carmichael up from his home in Victoria Terrace, so that they could go straight to the hospital. Falconer was in fine form and whistling a catchy number from 'The Pirates of Penzance' as he pulled up outside the sergeant's house.

'Morning, sir.'

Falconer's breathy melody hit an accidental F# as Carmichael opened the car door. What in the name of blue blazes was the lad wearing today? (Or should that have been 'blue blazers'?) This was a totally new combination – a bad taste confection whipped up to rot the wisdom tooth of elegant attire. Falconer's eyes took unbelieving note: shorts, in black-watch tartan; shirt, in bishops' purple; socks, fluorescent orange; trainers, yellow.

Seeing the attention his appearance had drawn, Carmichael smiled. 'Do you like it, sir? All new. Me mum got it for me down the market yesterday. She says it's ever so cheerful and I think so too.'

'It's absolutely unique,' replied the inspector truthfully, thereby dodging the prickly issue. There was no kind way he could give his real opinion. Maybe colour blindness ran in the family.

II

Dorothy Manningford had regained consciousness in the early hours of the morning, and they found her slightly propped up in her bed and dozing. As they entered the room, she stirred and acknowledged their presence with a movement of the fingers of her left hand, in which there was still attached a drip needle.

She had been moved from the ITU and was now in a private room, a much more cheerful and less de-humanised place than that in which they had last seen her. The flooring was still in an easily mopped material, but pictures hung on the walls, and a television set squatted at the end of her bed, should she feel up to its dubious offerings in the name of entertainment.

'I rather hoped I'd be seeing you soon,' she greeted them, lucid, although she sounded very weary.

'How are you feeling?' It was a daft question, as Falconer realised almost before the words had left his mouth, but he could think of nothing more suitable to say.

'Pretty much as bad as I probably look. They haven't allowed me a mirror yet.'

'I'm sorry. Sorry to disturb you too, but I need to ask if you can remember anything about yesterday and your accident.'

'It's all right, Inspector, no need to worry about amnesia. I can remember everything right up to when the car left the road.'

'We got a report back on the car. Your brake pipes had been cut, so I'm afraid to inform you that it was no accident. It was deliberate.'

'I know.'

'You do?'

'Yes.'

'How?'

'I'd better start from the beginning. Are you ready to take this down, Sergeant?' and, as she looked properly at Carmichael for the first time, her eyes widened slightly.

'Are you OK, Mrs Manningford?' he asked with concern in his voice.

'I'm fine, Sergeant. I was just wondering exactly how bruised I am under all these dressings.'

Falconer put a hand over his mouth to suppress a smile, but the meaning of her words went right over Carmichael's head as he perched on a chair by her bedside, pen poised, waiting to take notes.

'First, I want to put a few things straight about Piers and me,' she began. 'You've only ever seen us bicker and quarrel and you, as well as most other people, probably think I don't care for him, but that's not the case at all. In fact it's the exact opposite. I adore my husband – at least I did – and with me being older than him, I've always been worried that he'd find someone else, someone younger. But I didn't dare show my concern, for I knew he'd take advantage of it. That's how we've ended up like we have.

'I've always treated him harshly, trying to keep him keen, hoping it wasn't just my money he wanted. And even if it was, money is power, so I thought that all the while I kept control of my own money, I would have the power to hang on to him. It sounds rather pathetic when I put it into words,

239

but that's just how things were. But the money wasn't enough, was it? He did find someone else, someone younger, and so conveniently just next door. I'd lost, and couldn't even see it. I must have seemed such a fool to everyone else.'

'Don't be so harsh on yourself, Mrs Manningford. He tried to kill you, after all.'

'No, he didn't.'

'He cut your brake pipes, knowing that you'd fly off like that. That's attempted murder.'

'I cut those brake pipes, inspector.'

'You did?'

'Yes.'

'But why?'

She stopped to gather her thoughts and continued, 'When I knew what had been going on, there didn't seem to be much to live for and I wanted revenge. It seemed like an awfully good idea at the time, to cut the pipes and drive hell for leather until the inevitable happened. I didn't want to carry on living, and if anything happened to me, I wanted him to be held responsible. I actually wanted him to be found guilty of my murder. I wanted to blight his life the way he had blighted mine.'

'So you just drove off and put your foot down?'

'Yes. Then, when I lost control of the car, I instinctively fought it, but I couldn't do anything: it was too late. And the next thing I remember is waking up here and being rather glad that I wasn't dead.'

'So your husband had nothing to do with this?'

'That's right. Absolutely nothing. This one's all down to me, I'm afraid.'

Falconer was beginning to feel a little light-headed. 'What about the Sunday night that Reg Morley was murdered? You said your husband didn't go out of the house. Do you still stand by that statement?'

'Of course I do. When we're not arguing, ours is a very quiet household – no children, no pets: nothing much to make a noise except ourselves.'

Here she stopped and her eyes widened again, making her bruised face wince with pain. 'You surely don't think that Piers had anything to do with those murders, do you?' She looked incredulous. 'The man's a coward at heart. He wouldn't – couldn't – do anything like that.'

'Not even to protect his own interests?'

She tried to shake her head, but failed. 'Not even to save his own skin. His weapons are words and wheedling and creeping. Whatever came out, he'd try to talk his way out of it, persuade me it wasn't his fault, that he'd been led astray. Believe me, Inspector, that man doesn't know how to be violent. That was patently obvious when I caught him with his bit on the side, in that so-called studio of hers. He didn't lift a hand to defend himself, or her.

'I'd even gone so far as to think about how things would be if I survived the accident: how it might even strengthen our marriage, or at least give me another hold over him. I thought it might at least have brought him to my bedside.'

'I'm afraid we're responsible for keeping him from being here, Mrs Manningford. He's in custody.'

'Arrested?' She closed her eyes for a moment as

241

tears began to trickle down her cheeks. 'That's rich. Well, you've got the wrong man, Inspector. And do you know,' she said, brightening just a little, 'I rather think you can keep him. Maybe I'm the one who's been brought to their senses.'

III

Falconer had arranged for Piers Manningford's release from custody. The case against him had collapsed with Dorothy's admissions, and Falconer had no further grounds for holding him, if what Dorothy had told him about that Sunday night was true. He had no reason to suspect otherwise, was unable to conceive that she was playing a bluff, in her frail state. He simply could not see this as another inter-marital power struggle in their ailing relationship. In their closing moments with her he had felt that although Dorothy was still alive, her marriage had nonetheless died with her survival.

Chapter Twenty-three

Tuesday 21st July – morning

I

Tuesday had dawned overcast and humid, a dull day that had lost none of the heat of its predecessors, but was airless and oppressive, with a depressing atmosphere that suited Harry Falconer's mood, as he tried to come to terms with the collapse of his case. He felt crushed by the thought that he was right back to square one, and was sitting moodily at his desk staring balefully into space, when Carmichael made his appearance.

'Where the hell have you been, Carmichael?' he snapped, venting his spleen on his subordinate. 'Have you seen the time?'

'Sorry, sir.' The younger man apologised, walking carefully towards his desk. 'Not feeling quite a hundred per cent.'

Falconer looked up, at the hollow tone of his sergeant's voice. He did not look a hundred per cent either. His clothes were the same as he had worn the day before, but his skin seemed to have changed tone in sympathy with his bright apparel, and his face had a greenish tinge, his eyes were hollow and dark ringed, and a slick of sweat covered his forehead.

'Whatever's wrong with you?' Falconer barked,

still sulking. 'You look like a crock of shit!'

'Thanks, sir. That's just about how I feel. I had a kebab last night from Mickey the Snack's van. Must've been a dodgy one. I've been up all night. If it's not been one end, it's been the other. Shat through the eye of a needle, I have,' he finished descriptively.

'OK, OK. Thanks for painting a picture for me. Are you sure you're up to being here?'

'I'll be fine. I managed a cup of tea this morning, and I haven't chucked since about seven. Anyway, I'll feel better keeping busy.'

'If you're sure.'

'I'm OK. I'll just sit down for a while, though. My head's going round a bit, but I'll be better with something to do.'

Falconer left him to it and lapsed back into his brown study for the best part of a quarter of an hour, coming to terms with the fact that he would have to go back to Castle Farthing and start doing the rounds all over again. His nagging instinct that he had missed something seemed to have been right, and he would just have to poke, pry and question until he discovered the missing piece of the puzzle.

II

Falconer drove slowly and carefully that morning, using Carmichael's face as a barometer. The last thing he wanted in his car was the sort of pollution that the sergeant had been producing, courtesy of Mickey the Snack, whoever he might be.

With a conscious decision to distract his under-the-weather companion, he decided that they would start their enquiries at Jasmine Cottage, as the sight of Kerry Long always seemed to have a cheering influence on him. Their knock, however, brought no response and, checking his watch, Falconer muttered a silent curse. How stupid of him. It was mid-morning on a weekday. She would be at work of course.

'Come along, Carmichael. She'll be at Allsorts. Let's get ourselves over there.'

'OK, but don't walk too fast, sir.'

'In this humidity? Do you think I'm mad?'

There was a queue in the shop and Falconer joined the end of it, as there seemed to be no sign of Kerry Long, just Rosemary Wilson ringing up goods at the till and stopping for a chat with each of her customers.

Carmichael shuffled dejectedly round the shelves, once more examining the extraordinary mix of goods on display. One short length of wall alone held babies' dummies, staples, cocktail sticks, fire-lighters, shoelaces in a variety of colours, hairnets, and sealing wax. The walrus and the carpenter would have had a field day in here. Occasionally the sergeant stopped as his stomach cramped and a wave of nausea washed over him. The hot, airless interior was beginning to make him feel dizzy again.

Falconer, meanwhile, working his way to the head of the queue, had searched in a bored manner through his pockets, hoping to surprise an uneaten mint, and finding instead that odd coin that had been found by Carmichael in the back

245

garden of Crabapple Cottage, something that he had still not remembered to add to the evidence bag for Reg Morley's murder. In a distracted manner he took it out and began to flip it over in his hand as he finally reached the counter.

'Good morning, Mrs Wilson. Is your niece about? We'd like a word, if possible.' And right this minute, he thought, having already wasted enough time listening to enquiries about relatives, ailments, relatives' ailments, the state of the country, and garden pests.

'She's not here I'm afraid, Inspector.'

'Well, she's not at home. We've already tried there.' Really, this case was just one wild goose chase after another. Making any headway was proving as difficult as trying to nail jelly to the ceiling, or knit fog.

'No, I know she's not there. There's been a bit of trouble.'

'What sort of trouble?' asked Falconer, continuing to play with the coin, one eye on Carmichael who had found a few bare inches of wall and was drooping against it looking very unhappy.

'It started with Buster – you know, old Morley's dog that Martha Cadogan took in. Well, he must have got out somehow first thing this morning, and come trotting on down to his old home out of force of habit. Kerry's two kiddies had finished their breakfast and gone out with their toast crusts for the ducks – they're quite safe outside their own home, and it gives Kerry a few minutes to herself to clear away the dishes and get herself ready for work,' she added defensively, daring him to question her niece's maternal devotion.

'Of course, once they saw the dog that was it; they were all over him, patting him and stroking him and making a right fuss of him. He must have got all over-excited at so much attention and nipped young Kyle. He didn't mean no harm, I'm sure. He was just playing, and he didn't break the skin or anything, but how that child howled. Frightened, I suppose. Luckily the Brigadier happened along then, out for his "early morning constitutional" as he calls it. He grabbed Buster, delivered the children home, then took the dog back to Martha, who would've been frantic with worry if she'd realised he'd got out.'

This could prove to be a long day, thought Falconer, as he tried to hasten things along. 'So where is your niece? Has she gone to the doctor's or the hospital?'

'Good heavens, no. I said there was no real harm done. Both kiddies went into school as usual – it's the end of term and they didn't want to miss out on any of the fun – although Kyle insisted on a big bandage to advertise his mishap.

'No, Kerry had been that cross about the whole thing – she's never liked that dog as you know – and when she came into work she just worked herself into a right old state about it; how it could've been much worse, and how she thought the animal was a danger to children. She said it ought to be put down before it really hurt some-one, and she was going to give Martha a piece of her mind for letting it get loose in the first place. All wound up like a spring she was, and in the end I could do nothing with her and had to let her go and have her say. She won't get anywhere, though. Martha Cadogan won't have a bad word said about any animal, let alone her beloved Buster. Why, she's more fond of animals than she is of people, if you ask me. Might even account for her still being a spinster, I suppose.'

Falconer was beginning to get a fuzzy feeling in his head, like bad reception, but it had stirred his policeman's instinct, and he let the rest of her outpouring flow over him, his hand still unconsciously flipping the coin. He did not even notice Lillian Swainton-Smythe enter the shop, her eyes immediately becoming glued to the disc of metal that turned over and over in his hand, and it was not until she spoke that he became aware of her presence.

'Oh, I see you've found Auntie's lucky coin. She will be pleased. Where on earth was it? She's looked everywhere for it, even had Bertie send up a prayer to St Anthony for its safe return.'

At these words, what he had been missing clarified for Falconer and, as the mental penny dropped, so did the physical coin, his hand misjudging the catch in his realisation of what must have really happened.

'This is your Aunt Martha's coin?' he asked as he bent to retrieve it.

'Yes. She calls it her lucky coin. She's been awfully upset at losing it. It's an old co-operative coin she's had for donkeys' years. One of those Anglesey pennies. Always keeps it in her bag.'

But Falconer had stopped listening. *Animals!* That was what this case was about, and had been all along, not people. Animals had been the thread that had run through both murders, and he had been too blind, or too stupid, to see it.

He had even said himself that the old lady was obsessed with animals, had helped her pick up her shopping when she had been buying food for the feral cats, the hedgehogs and the birds in her garden. He had listened to her wittering on about wildlife in general, and had heard her harsh words for both Reg Morley and his great-nephew. And none of it had sunk into his stupid, stupid brain.

Good grief, he had even been there as an eyewitness when the woman was mending her trellis with wire – the wire which had choked the two victims, probably cut from the same roll! – and he had been too blind to see what had, literally, been right before his eyes.

Reg Morley, apart from being a despicable specimen of humanity, had treated Buster harshly. Mike Lowry had shot and poisoned rats and stray cats, then he had foolishly decided to take his temper out on Buster and kicked him. That must have been the last straw for the old lady, as far as she was concerned.

Martha Cadogan had admitted that she had phoned the vicarage on the night of the latter's murder to see if all was well. What if what she had been doing, in reality, was making sure that Lowry was on his own and out cold. It must have been she who was responsible for doping them both, though at this point he had no idea how, and no time to ponder on it.

These deaths had nothing to do with greed, or adultery, or any of the number of possible motives that he had pursued so avidly in his blind, blundering quest for the truth. The real motive was so simple, it had gone straight over his head. That sweet little old lady had killed because of what two men had done to dumb animals, and one dumb animal in particular, and now Kerry Long had gone to see her to tell her she thought Buster ought to be destroyed. If he was right about this, that young woman was in real danger.

III

Pausing only to grab a whey-faced Carmichael, he asked if there was a gate from the back of the shop to the rear access road. Receiving an answer in the affirmative, he pushed his way through the stock room without explanation, practically dragging Carmichael in his wake. There was no time to take the car. They would have to go on foot and hope they were in time.

As they ran, Falconer explained his revelation as briefly and as succinctly as he could, and the sergeant's face contorted with worry as he put on an extra spurt of speed, despite his indisposition.

It was with little difficulty that they found the gate at the back of The Old School House, the very same one that Martha Cadogan had used to put out her rubbish the night she had caught Reg Morley fleeing from spying on Rebecca Rollason.

'What if we're too late, sir?' Carmichael looked frantic.

'And what if we're not,' Falconer rationalised. 'Now, let's take this calmly when we get to them. If nothing's happened yet, we don't want to spook the old dear. We'll let her think this is just another routine enquiry and see how things go.'

'And if something's already happened?' Car-michael swallowed convulsively and closed his eyes. He was already feeling dreadful, and the thought that something might have happened to Kerry made fresh waves of nausea wash over him.

'We'll cross that bridge when we come to it. Now, I'm going to open the gate, and let's just be nice and calm, completely normal, until we can see what we're dealing with.'

As they entered the garden they could see two figures sitting at the white wrought-iron table on the lawn. Between them was a tray holding a half-empty jug of lemonade and two full tumblers.

'Hello, gentlemen,' Martha greeted them, looking up. 'Have you been ringing the bell and I haven't heard you?'

This was a much better scenario than Falconer could have hoped for, and they approached the two women slowly, outwardly at their ease. Mar-tha Cadogan sat upright, as was her custom, her capacious bag by her chair, and smiled as they walked towards her. Kerry Long was dabbing at her eyes with a tissue, but Falconer only had eyes for the twin tumblers on the tray. Carmichael's attention was, to his dismay, split between concern for the younger woman's welfare and his own deteriorating physical condition. He was sweating freely now and dizziness almost overwhelmed him.

They were within a few feet of the table when Kerry reached out a hand for her glass of lemon-ade and Falconer was galvanised into action.

251

With a cry of, 'Don't drink that!' he lunged forward and dashed the glass from her hand.

Martha Cadogan's actions were just as fleet. In one fluid movement, unexpected in one of such age, she had reached into her bag and now stood before them, holding, at chest height, a venerable service revolver. Falconer and Carmichael froze; Kerry looked on appalled, her hand still outstretched, reaching for the glass that now lay on its side on the grass beside her chair.

'Don't move, any of you,' Martha commanded. 'This is my father's gun from the Great War. It may be old,' she explained, 'but I've kept it well-oiled and in use all these years.' Her voice had the same quiet, reasonable tone that she must have used in all those years of teaching, just making the situation even more bizarre.

'I often carry it in case I come across a creature in the woods that needs an end to its misery. They still set traps around here, you know,' she continued almost conversationally. 'On one occasion I even found a wounded deer. You can't just knock a creature of that size on the head with a stone. So I've kept Daddy's revolver in good condition and I've used it when necessary. Don't be foolish enough to think that I will be afraid to use it now.'

Carmichael had heard her clearly up to the mention of the deer, and then his own body had turned on him. His bowels cramped viciously as another wave of nausea swept over him. His dizziness heightened, he heard as if through cotton wool, and the scene before him bleached of colour, until it was monochrome and beginning to blur.

As the old lady uttered her last sentence the sergeant, in complete silence, dropped his not inconsiderable length across her in a dead faint, knocking her to the ground as he did so. As a surprise attack it was perfect, taking both attacker and victim with the same degree of surprise.

The gun fell from her grasp un-discharged, and Falconer sprang forward, retrieving first the weapon, then advancing upon the old lady who was firmly pinned to the ground under Carmichael's bulk, and sufficiently winded to have no strength left with which to struggle. His actions were not aided by Buster, who contributed to the melee by dancing around the prone figures barking, and the inspector called quite roughly for Kerry to pull him off and shut him in the house.

It was several minutes before an order of sorts was restored. Falconer had retrieved Kerry's glass, a few drops of liquid still retained in it, and put it aside for forensic analysis, doing the same with the other tumbler and jug just to be on the safe side. The revolver, which he had wrapped carefully in his handkerchief, now made an inelegant bulge in his jacket pocket.

Carmichael, he had unceremoniously pulled to his feet and assisted him to a chair, to repeat the process with his felled victim, despatching Kerry once more into the kitchen for glasses of water, while he made a call on his mobile phone for a car to collect Miss Cadogan.

His sergeant sat huffing and puffing like a grampus, as he fought for an acceptable level of awareness, and it was Martha who seemed to make a quicker recovery. 'I know you're going to

253

take me to the police station, Inspector, but would you be so kind as to let me collect a handkerchief first?'

'I shall accompany you to see that is all that you do,' agreed Falconer, marvelling at the fact that, in these circumstances, the old lady should still hold true to her upbringing and not want to leave the house without something on which to blow her nose. He only hoped she did not want to change into fresh bloomers, with him as a reluctant witness.

She was still a little shaky after her fall, and he offered her his arm as he led her into the house and upstairs. Her bedroom, when they reached it, was exactly as he would have imagined it: rag rugs on the floor, hand-sewn patchwork quilt on the old high dark wood frame of the bed, a sampler hanging above its headboard that read *Suffer the little children to come unto me*. The room smelt of lavender, and transported him back to the room that his grandmother had slept in when he was a boy.

'It's in the washstand drawer by the bed, Inspector. Do you want to open the drawer first?' Goodness, she was on the ball, and here he was, awash with nostalgia.

'Thank you, I will, Miss Cadogan, just to make sure there's nothing unexpected in there.'

From the drawer's depths Martha extracted a white lace-edged handkerchief with the initials MC embroidered in red in one corner. Falconer had expected the handkerchief to be pristine, and it was creased and stiff; not used, but somehow not fresh. Seeing his gaze, she smiled softly.

'Starched but, alas, un-ironed, Inspector. A rare moment of laziness which I'm sure you'll forgive, given the circumstances.'

Embarrassed, he nodded agreement, and turned away as she tucked it into her upper under-garments for safekeeping.

'I think it's time to go now,' he said, hearing a car pull up outside. 'I'll send the sergeant home with Ms Long and I'll come in the car with you if you like.'

'Thank you very much, young man, but can you do one more thing for me before we go?'

'What's that?'

'Can you arrange for Lillian to collect Buster and his bits and pieces. He can't stay here on his own, and someone will have to look after him while I'm away.'

IV

A call to the vicarage alerted Bertie Swainton-Smythe to the current situation and he agreed to collect Buster immediately, then tackle the difficult task of explaining to Lillian that her aunt had been arrested for murder. That sounded like a litre-of-gin task to Falconer, and he sent up a silent prayer for the vicar as he ended the call.

Falconer dispatched Carmichael and Kerry Long to Jasmine Cottage for a statement to be taken, explaining that he would travel in the offi-cial car with the old lady.

'What about your car, sir? It's parked in the vil-lage.'

Despite the heat Falconer shivered, blanched and swallowed hard, facing up to the reality of what was being suggested. 'You'll have to drive it back to the station, Sergeant,' and he handed over the keys with a heavy heart. 'You will be gentle with her, won't you?'

'Course, sir. Be a fair treat to drive a beast like that. Bet she goes like the clappers.'

'Not on a first date, Carmichael. Not on a first date, so be warned.'

Chapter Twenty-four

Tuesday 21st July – late afternoon

I

Martha Cadogan was perfectly prepared to make a full statement, and sat now in an interview room opposite Falconer as he explained the recording procedure to her. Behind her and beside the door, sat Acting DS Carmichael, returned from Castle Farthing and looking a good deal better than he had that morning. No doubt a good blast through the country lanes in someone else's pride and joy had had something to do with that, thought Falconer darkly, as he prepared to switch on the recording equipment.

'Before we begin, Inspector, do you think I may have what you might call a last request?'

He checked the movement of his hand and

asked, 'What sort of request?'

'Well, I've never smoked in my life, but I've seen things like this in television programmes. Do you think I might have a cigarette to try? It's hardly likely to do me any harm at my great age, and it would satisfy a curiosity of mine.'

'I'm sure that can be arranged,' Falconer demurred, surprised. Carmichael was duly sent off to persuade Bob Bryant from the front desk to part with one of his beloved comforters, and to escort Miss Cadogan out to the dedicated smoking area (otherwise known as 'round the back of the canteen'). A few minutes later, Falconer switched on the twin cassette-recorder, said his frontispiece and Martha, coughing slightly from her one unsuccessful flirtation with tobacco, began to speak.

'Of course, you know now that I was responsible for both of those deaths.'

'The deaths of Reginald Morley of Crabapple Cottage, High Street, Castle Farthing, and Michael Lowry of Castle Farthing Garage, Drovers Lane, Castle Farthing,' Falconer clarified, speaking directly to tape.

'I drugged them with sleeping tablets first, you know, so they wouldn't struggle. I'm not strong, and I couldn't have managed if they'd fought back.'

'Where did you get the sleeping tablets, Miss Cadogan?' At least that would be one little mystery cleared up.

'They were prescribed for a very old friend of mine, Evelyn Prendergast; we've known each other since we were children. I went up to Nottingham to nurse her through her last illness, just after New Year. Like me, she never married, and had no family who could help, and she had always been a good friend to me. It was the least I could do.

'It was cancer of course, and it had spread all over her body. She didn't want to die in a hospice amongst strangers, so I went and did what I could, and the Macmillan nurse came round and did what I couldn't. She'd had a new prescription filled for sleeping tablets when the pain suddenly got much worse, and she was given large doses of morphine round the clock and didn't need them any more. She only lasted a few days after that and, although I meant to hand the pills into the chemist, I somehow didn't get round to it.'

'These were diazepam tablets?'

'That's right. I understand they can be quite addictive, but that hardly mattered in Evelyn's case. Any addiction was doomed to be short-lived, given her state of health.

'Anyway, I brought them back with me; thought I might need some help sleeping after losing my oldest friend – we went to school together in the village you know, before her family moved north. Anyway, I took one – felt awful the next day – then thought I might put them to better use helping sick or injured animals out of their pain and suffering. I always felt a bit awkward using Daddy's gun, and this would be just like going to sleep for them, so I always carried a few of them dissolved in water (with a little sugar to take away the bitterness) in a little pill bottle in my bag.'

Even the shock of being discovered as a murderess had not deflected the old lady's thoughts from her concerns for animal welfare, thought Falconer ruefully.

'I also carried a length of wire with me. Small animals caught in traps are too much for my old hands, but I could still help them out of their misery with a loop of wire.'

'If we might return to the two human deaths, Miss Cadogan.'

'Of course. I'm sorry. I'm just trying to explain how it came about that I had the means with me in my bag that Sunday evening.'

'What made you decide on that particular day to do something like that?'

'To murder him? Oh, it could have been for any number of reasons, as you know, on any day, but that particular day I'd seen him tug and tug at poor Buster's lead, dragging him along half-choked, and I saw red. It was like a bomb going off in my head, and I just decided that that was the last time that man would ever inflict suffering on another living creature.

'But I didn't rush into it. I bided my time, and walked back to the village at about half past eleven. It was always quiet by that time on a Sunday night, and if anyone saw me they'd assume I was off to see the badgers in the wood, or out looking for strays. I wasn't in the least worried or nervous.

'I knocked on his door and he just let me in; seemed in a rare good mood and pleased to have someone to talk to, about whatever had cheered him so. He started prattling on, I noticed he had milk heating on the stove, and it seemed as if everything had been set up ready for me: as if it were meant.

'He didn't turn a hair when I offered to make his cocoa. It was almost too easy. Cocoa's a bitter drink, and Reg had smoked most of his life and was always complaining that nothing had any taste any more. I just poured the contents of my little bottle into his drink and sat with him until he'd talked himself to sleep. Then I wrapped the wire round his neck and pulled as hard as I could, and then twisted it. Dear little Buster never stirred; he's always had a soft spot for me.'

'About the wire, Miss Cadogan,' began Falconer.

'Oh yes, before I forget, you'll find the rest of the roll in my garden shed. I'm afraid you won't be able to get a match on the cut end, because I was using some of it to mend the trellis when you called on Saturday afternoon. Do you remember? You were kind enough to pass me the pliers to cut it.'

Falconer remembered, and blushed that vital evidence had sat under his very nose, unrecognised for what it was.

'I'd like to show you something, Miss Cadogan,' the inspector said, feeling in his jacket pocket. 'Would you tell me if you recognise this?' and he opened his hand to reveal the coin that had proved to be the key to unravelling the whole sorry chain of events for him.

Her face lit up. 'Why, it's my lucky coin, Inspector. Where on earth did you find it? I've had it since I was a girl – found it up at the old castle ruins playing digging for buried treasure. I must have been about six years old.'

'Sergeant Carmichael found it outside, at the back of Mr Morley's cottage.'

'May I have it back?'

'Not yet, I'm afraid. Can you tell me how it came to be where it was found?'

'Of course,' she remembered. 'When I knew Reg was quite dead I got up to leave and little Buster was so eager to come with me. I told him I'd be back for him the very next day, but I had such a struggle keeping him in and getting the door shut, that I dropped my bag. I thought I'd picked up everything, but that must have been when I lost it. I didn't miss it for a day or two, so I couldn't be sure just when it had gone astray, and I'd quite forgotten dropping my bag like that till now.'

'Shall we move on to the death of Michael Lowry now?'

'That nasty boy! He was getting quite as bad as Reg. Why, the way he spoke to me on Wednesday morning last, and the way he attacked my poor Buster – he kicked him you know; really bruised his ribs. Well, that was almost the last straw.

'I had everything I needed in my bag that evening at Mr Romaine's birthday celebrations – Lillian even chided me for bringing such a bulky article with me, but I told her I was too old for such nonsense as evening bags – and even then I wasn't sure I was going to go through with it. And then that beastly boy started in on just about everyone there, accusing them of all sorts of things, just like his great-uncle. That's when I knew that I was going to go through with it. He had to go too.'

A small smile played at the corners of her

261

mouth as she said this last, and Falconer's blood ran cold at her lack of remorse.

'I decided I'd put him out of everyone else's misery, so to speak,' she continued. 'I chose my moment and went to the bar to buy a round of drinks, making sure that I took my bag with me. I palmed the bottle as I took out my purse.

'That Michael Lowry had put his pint of beer on the bar and was laying about him with that evil tongue of his. No one took any notice of me: they were all looking at him. It's really amazing what you can get away with if you're audacious enough about it. I just slipped off the top, held my hand over his glass, and the deed was done.'

Falconer whistled through his teeth. Just like a conjuror, he thought. Distract the audience and the quickness of the hand deceives the eye.

'And that was everything put into motion, Inspector. I called to check that Bertie had got home – I hardly wanted to run into him, with what I had in mind, did I? And about midnight I slipped out the back way. The only time I was in the open was crossing Drovers Lane, and the rest of the village was asleep by then.'

If only you knew, Falconer thought. That particular night, Castle Farthing was positively alive with furtive figures creeping about. If she had come by way of the village centre, she would have found it positively crawling with people.

'And that was it. I let myself in – I knew Bertie couldn't have secured the door – slipped my little piece of wire round his neck, and then he was dead too.'

By the time Martha Cadogan had finished mak-

262

ing her statement, afternoon had become evening and, as they escorted her back to her 'room' (as she called it), she asked if she could have a glass of water, as she often got thirsty in the night.

Falconer agreed without hesitation, although he forbore to add that it would be a plastic mug of water. Glass was much too dangerous a substance to be allowed to prisoners in custody.

As they left her, Carmichael asked, 'What will happen to her, sir? She's so old. And she doesn't even seem to care about what she's done.'

'God knows, Carmichael. I certainly don't. I'm just glad it's out of our hands now.'

II

Martha Cadogan lay down on her hard bunk mattress and waited until someone had opened the spy-hole in the door and checked her, the picture of a sweet old lady asleep.

As the footsteps moved away, she extracted from her undergarments the stiff, crumpled handkerchief she had collected earlier from her bedroom, in anticipation of this moment. This she inserted into her mug of water, stirring it with her fingers for a good couple of minutes, watching the water turn cloudy. Finally, she extracted the small piece of material, wrung it out over the mug, and placed it tidily over the end of the bunk frame to dry, tidy to the end.

Really, she thought, it had been most useful watching that documentary on the various and imaginative ways in which people smuggled drugs

263

into the country. Little bottles weren't the only vehicle in which one could transport oblivion, and it had given her the chance to be prepared. Lifting the mug to her lips, she drank until it was empty, then laid down, ready to meet her maker.

Life was declared extinct by the police surgeon the following morning, when the duty officer had failed to rouse her.

Epilogue

Autumn

I

The leaves in the hedgerows and on the trees in Castle Farthing had turned through their annual rainbow and were beginning to fall.

Outside the vicarage sat a removal truck, furniture being transferred to its cavernous inside by the usual motley crew of removal men: a very fat man, a very wizened old man, and a tall, gangling youth still wearing a veritable bandit's mask of acne. A figure in black darted back and forth, exhorting them to be careful of this item, to take great care not to drop that.

In the churchyard a middle-aged woman wandered between the rows of gravestones, a small dog at her heels. Occasionally she would stop and read, her lips moving silently.

Below his wife Norma's name and dates she read:

REGINALD ERNEST MORLEY
Born 11th April 1926 Died 13th July 2009.
RIP

A few steps further on she halted again:

MICHAEL SHANE LOWRY
Husband of Kerry and father of Dean and Kyle
Born 9th October 1979. Died 16th July 2009.
MUCH MISSED

She moved on, the dog darting off now and again to investigate tantalising smells and interesting rustles in the undergrowth. At the other side of the churchyard she stopped for a third and final time to read:

MARTHA WINIFRED CADOGAN
Born 7th March 1924. Died 22nd July 2009.
THE LORD IS MY SHEPHERD

She raised a hand to wipe away a stray tear, as a figure in clerical garb approached her. 'Don't up-set yourself, Lillian my dear. It's best we're going. Too many painful memories here. Come along, it's almost time. Pastures new and all that.'
   'Poor Auntie.'
   'God was merciful, Lillian. Even if she had lived, the brain tumour they found would have killed her before she stood trial: you know that. And her con-dition does go some way to explaining her beha-

265

viour. She was used to putting down sick and injured animals. In her altered mental state, she probably just saw it as putting down sick and flawed people.'

'How can you be so charitable, Bertie? What about "Thou shalt not kill"?'

'What about "To err is human, to forgive is divine"? Aunt Martha was ill, and God will forgive her. He is infinite in his mercy, and all we mere mortals can do is accept that. At least we're taking good care of Buster. She'd have been pleased about that. Now, do you fancy a last cup of tea before we get underway?'

'Please, Bertie.'

Lillian Swainton-Smythe had not touched alcohol since her aunt's death.

II

Dean and Kyle Lowry were out in the back garden of Jasmine Cottage, shrieking with delight as they chased the falling autumn leaves around.

Kerry Long now owned the cottage. With the help of her godfather's solicitor, her husband's estate had passed to her, along with the deeds of the property next door. This last, along with the garage lease and contents, had been sold, and the proceeds, together with the cash and insurance indirectly inherited from Mike's detested great-uncle, had allowed her to purchase Jasmine Cottage. After covering the outstanding funeral expenses, she had even been left with a small nest egg to invest for her family's future.

She was glad the children were so absorbed in their game, chasing around outside and tiring themselves out. She would like a bit of peace and quiet that evening.

Delicious smells wafted from the kitchen and made her smile, as she laid the table in the small dining room. Two candles sat in squat glass holders, one at each end of the table, a posy of short-stemmed, rust-coloured chrysanthemums in the middle. She was looking forward to the meal she had planned for that evening, and the children would be so pleased to see Uncle Davey again. He had been like a rock, such a support to all three of them since that terrifying morning in the garden of The Old School House.

III

In the centre of the village, the general store Allsorts was just shutting up shop for the day, as The Fisherman's Flies opened its doors to another evening's trade.

The sun was low in the sky and on the green Tristram Rollason was taking his evening constitutional, running round and round the pond shouting 'quack' and flapping his arms at the alarmed ducks, watched fondly from the nearby bench by his mother.

In the garden of Pilgrims' Rest, Dorothy Manningford was taking a last walk round the garden before locking up for the evening. She still walked with a limp, a legacy of her accident that would be with her for some time yet, and the ankle and arm she had broken ached on damp days but, overall, she was content. She had got used to life on her own since Piers had moved in with his cousin Bruce, and she relished the peace and freedom she had gained, however painful that transition had been.

There had been other changes, too, in Castle Farthing. The Romaines had left the village, and the flagstaff of a 'for sale' sign stood to attention in the front garden of their property.

Crabapple Cottage had been bought by a couple of 'townies' with two golden retrievers, as a weekend retreat. Appalled at its primitive interior, they intended to gut it and rename it 'The Hideaway'. Thus, it was empty most of the time, affording Dean and Kyle Long the chance to play unchastised and to relish their continued freedom.

The garage in Drovers Lane stood empty, awaiting redevelopment by a large oil company, the nearest source of petrol now situated in Steynham St Michael some three and a half miles away and a temporary but unwelcome inconvenience to many.

Village life rolled relentlessly on, without heed of its victims or their fates. All was pretty, all was serene, as it always had been; as it always would be: on the surface.

At The Old Manor House, Brigadier Malpas-Graves surveyed the borders of wallflowers he had planted out a few days ago.

'I say, Joyce,' he called. 'Something's been digging in this corner – something quite big. You don't suppose it's one of those damned dogs from old Morley's place, do you?'

The publishers hope that this book has given you enjoyable reading. Large Print Books are especially designed to be as easy to see and hold as possible. If you wish a complete list of our books please ask at your local library or write directly to:

Magna Large Print Books
Magna House, Long Preston,
Skipton, North Yorkshire.
BD23 4ND